Windward Island

by Karleen Bradford

Kids Can Press Ltd.
Toronto

Kids Can Press Ltd. acknowledges with appreciation the assistance of the Canada Council and the Ontario Arts Council in the production of this book.

Canadian Cataloguing in Publication Data
Bradford, Karleen
  Windward island

ISBN 0-921103-75-1

I. Title.

PS8553.R217W5 1989 jC813'.54 C89-094342-7
PZ7.B73Wi 1989

Printed and bound in Canada by Webcom Ltd.

Edited by Charis Wahl
Typeset by Pixel Graphics Inc.
Cover design by N.R. Jackson

89 0 9 8 7 6 5 4 3 2

Acknowledgements

I would like to thank the Canada Council for the assistance that allowed me to do the research for this book.

I would also like to thank Sylvia and Walter Young for inviting me to live with them on their island for a time, and Peter Young, who taught me about it and showed me how to dig for mussels.

Finally, I would like to thank my agent, Nancy Colbert, and editor, Charis Wahl, for helping me to write a better book.

For Chris

Chapter 1

No MATTER HOW hard he tried, Loren couldn't shake the feeling of guilt that had been nagging him all day. He straightened up, heaved a sigh, and pushed a sweaty strand of dark brown hair out of his eyes. He'd put it off long enough. Today he had to tell Caleb.

He looked around one last time. It seemed there was already a musty, unused smell to the one-roomed building that had served as school to him for the last nine years. He moved over to the doorway. The walls were still book-lined, blackboard and maps still there, the few desks lined up neatly, as usual. Only the computer was missing. It had been sent back to Halifax with Mr. Henley the day before. Loren told himself he was just checking to make sure he had done a good job of cleaning, but he knew full well that he was really saying goodbye.

For more than sixty years the children of Windward Island had come here to learn whatever the Nova Scotia mainland teachers had been able to share with them. Some of the teachers, Caleb's mother among them, had stayed to marry and become islanders themselves. Now all that was finished. Loren Randall and Caleb Landry were the last two young people to finish grade nine here, the last two young people on the island. No teacher would be returning in the fall. From grade ten on, school was on the mainland, and the schoolhouse had served its purpose.

"Loren! Have you finished already?" Caleb raced up the dirt path, awkward in his heavy boots. "You're *some* fast! I was just coming to help you."

Loren jumped, startled, and quickly slammed the door shut behind himself. Always, he had shared everything with Caleb, but somehow today he couldn't share this — this ending of one whole part of his life.

"Well, if you're all done then, how about getting some mussels for a mussel bake tonight? The tide's out." Caleb's broad, freckled face was split in his usual good-natured grin. His short stubble of bright red hair gleamed in the sunlight. "And I've got some news, too," he added. "You'll never guess what's happened."

Loren hardly heard him. How would Caleb react to what he had to tell him? He'd hardly ever seen Caleb out of sorts. Usually, whenever Loren felt down or depressed, he could count on Caleb to joke him out of it, but not this time. He slipped his feet into the boots he'd left just outside the door and shrugged the thoughts away, at least for the moment. A mussel bake sounded like a good idea. He'd tell Caleb then.

They set off up the path, side by side. Caleb was shorter but he walked with such purposeful strides, chin jutting determinedly, that Loren had to lengthen his easier, loping gait to keep up. He still wasn't really listening as Caleb talked on beside him, but suddenly something caught his attention.

"...and they're coming *today*," Caleb was saying.

"What? Who's coming today?" Loren broke in.

Caleb retorted, "I knew you weren't listening. You've got that 'busy elsewhere' look on your face that you always get when you're off in your own world. I'll start over," he said with exaggerated patience. "Now this time, *listen* to me. Do you remember Mom telling us about her best friend from Halifax, who came here donkey's years ago to visit, and ended up marrying an island man and dragging him back to the mainland?"

"Yes...I guess..." Actually Loren didn't remember too much about the story other than what he had heard from the older folks. How could Dan Lohnes have given up everything — his whole life here on the island — and "run off," as they put it, to live in the city and work at some suffocating job? The fishing had been good back then. There had been a fortune in it. Not like now.

Caleb rushed on. "Mom got a telephone call last night from this man. It seems his wife — Mom's friend — was killed in a car accident. Way back last Christmas. Mom hadn't heard. Now he's going to come back here for the summer. He's going to open up his family place — you know, the old Lohnes house that's been deserted since before we were born?"

"That'll be some job." Loren was beginning to pay attention. "It must be a wreck in there."

"Yeah. Well, anyway, he's coming *today*. And that's not all..." Caleb paused, waiting for Loren's reaction.

"Okay," Loren answered obediently, "what else?"

"He's got a daughter. Same age as us. And he's bringing her. That should liven things up around here!"

"Here? For the whole summer?"

Caleb was gratified to see that he'd finally shaken Loren. "Here," he repeated. "For the whole summer."

Suddenly the summer, which Loren had seen stretching so predictably ahead of them, had gone askew. He had no wish at all to have things "livened up." He'd counted on having the next few months to bring Caleb around to the necessity of his decision. He'd counted on having those months to reassure himself that nothing was really going to change after all. But somebody new on the island...a girl their own age...

"Wonder what she'll be like?" Caleb mused. "City girl. She's never even visited the island." He seemed intrigued by the idea.

They stopped in the barn in Caleb's back yard to get two iron picks and a couple of buckets, then headed across the vegetable garden to the path that led through the trees and down to the shore. Loren deliberately let Caleb get a fair piece ahead. He looked up automatically to the lighthouse standing at the top of the hill. In the hard, bright sunlight he couldn't see the flashing light, but he knew it was on. It, like most of the other lighthouses along the coast and on the islands, was on twenty-four hours a day now. No "lighting up" in the evenings anymore, such as his father had described to him. As always, regret tugged at him. Progress, they called it. But how he wished he could have been lightkeeper here when the light had really needed tending. As his father had been in his youth, and *his* father before him. At least it wasn't fully automated yet, as most of the other lights were, and his father was still the lightkeeper. At least *he* hadn't been let go yet.

Caleb was through the narrow band of trees edging the cliffs and scrambling down the steep slate ramparts. Loren hurried to catch up. The tide was full out. They stumbled and slipped over the slimy, wrack-covered rocks, breathing in the salty tang, until they were almost at the water's edge. The wind was coming up from the southeast and the waves were getting restless.

"Why are they coming?" Loren called to Caleb's back.

"Don't know," Caleb shouted over his shoulder. "Mom didn't say."

"If he never wanted to come back before, why now?" Loren persisted, but Caleb's mind was on mussels.

"I'll start with this bunch here," he said as he waded out into the tide pools.

Loren chose a row of jagged rocks. They pulled back the kelp, exposing the clusters of blue-black mussels embedded in the leftover pools between the rocks, then dug at them with their picks. When they had harvested all the mussels under the first kelp, they moved on. They'd been mussel hunting like this all their lives, practically; there was no need for many words. By the time both buckets were almost full, the wind was making a fair lop on the waves.

Loren sat back on his heels for a moment and

looked out over the water. Idly, he noticed a lovely old Tancook schooner tacking just outside Old Grampus, the shoal off the lighthouse point. He could hear the doleful moans and plaints of the Groaner, the whistle buoy that marked the shoal. It was tossing in the rising seas, water rushing in and out of the hollow pipe that ran through it, causing the loud, soughing groans that gave the buoy its name. The schooner had all sails set, and the sight of her silhouetted against the late afternoon sun sent a thrill through him. Some day...

Two black ducks flew low across the water and disappeared swiftly around the point. A marsh hawk swooped out of Low Swamp, pursued by a crow with murder on its mind. Then they, too, disappeared into the trees. Loren bent to his work.

They had collected just about all the mussels they would need, and Loren was thinking about heading back, when suddenly Caleb shouted.

"The men are coming back, Loren. And look! There's a cruiser with them."

Loren looked up. A small fleet of fishing boats, strung out in a single file, was coming up fast. Just behind them was a sleek, powerful cruiser. Even as Loren watched, it overtook the slower craft and passed them. They skewed a bit in its wake, slowed, then came back up to full speed.

"That must be Dan Lohnes," Caleb yelled.

They gathered up all their gear and headed for the island harbour at a run, stumbling a little until they gained the comparatively good footing of the pebbly shore. They reached the wharf just as the cruiser was nosing in. One man was steering the boat while another stood in the stern with a coiled line, ready to leap out. When he saw Caleb waiting, he tossed the line to him. Loren caught hold of the bow and made the painter fast to a ringbolt on the wharf.

"Thank you kindly," the man in the stern called out to them. Then he clambered out. After cutting the engine and checking the switches, the other man followed.

The fishing boats reached the harbour entrance, with Caleb's father, Angus, in the lead boat. Old Uncle Lem Parker and his son, Clarence, followed, with Frank and young Frank Parker close behind. (At fifty years old, young Frank was called "young" only to distinguish him from his father.) Caleb's uncle, Forster Landry brought up the rear. For a few moments the small harbour was jammed with boats, but with Caleb and Loren's help each boat was soon hauled up on its slip and the men were gathering curiously around the visitors.

Caleb's father was a quiet, softspoken man, with the confident air of someone who knows what he has to do and that he does it well. He had, in common with all the other island men, a lined, weatherbeaten face and sharp, bright eyes that told of years of watching and searching and living with the sea. He walked up to the man who had tossed Caleb the stern line and held out his hand.

"Dan! It *is* you, isn't it?"

"Angus!" the other man exclaimed. "You haven't changed a bit! All these years…"

"Few grey hairs. Few more wrinkles. Sea's not too

kind to a man, you know."

"It's been good to you, Angus. You look fine. Real fine."

With a shock, Loren realized that the two men must be about the same age. Angus, in spite of his words, looked at least ten years younger. The other had the stooped, grey look of an old man and was making an obvious effort to be light-hearted. "Angus, let me introduce you to my good friend Greg Winters. He was kind enough to bring us over. And somewhere around here…," he looked back at the boat vaguely, "I have a very disgruntled daughter."

A girl came out of the cabin. Loren stared in amazement. She was dressed in expensive, well-fitting sports clothes, gleaming white from top to toe. Sea-green eyes looked out from a perfectly made-up but sullen face. Not a strand of her well-cut, soft brown hair was out of place.

She must have sat in the cabin the whole way over, Loren thought. Then he winced as she climbed out and over the well-polished deck planks in leather-soled shoes.

"Ah, April, come and meet my very old friend Angus Landry." She came reluctantly forward. Her father turned to the boys. "And is one of these helpful young men your son?"

Angus introduced Caleb and Loren, then the others. "Annie is looking forward to seeing you, Dan," he said. "And you, too, April. She and your mother were such good friends — all the time they were growing up…" He paused, then turned to Dan Lohnes. "She's pretty upset, though," he added in an undertone. "It was a shock."

14

"I know," Dan Lohnes replied. "I should have written...let her know somehow...it was just..." He turned away from Angus quickly and stared out to sea. All the hearty, friendly manner dropped away and he suddenly looked tired and deflated. "I couldn't, Angus. I couldn't write or talk to anyone. I couldn't do anything. I still can't." He turned back. The lines of pain in his face had deepened and his eyes looked dead. "I don't even know why we're here," he said, so softly that Loren barely heard him. "I don't know..."

"Well, that makes two of us."

Loren looked at April, shocked by the bitterness in her voice. There was an awkward silence. The other men suddenly remembered they had gear to stow away in the old fish storehouse by the wharf.

"Come on," Angus put in quickly. "We'll get you up to the house. Caleb will help with the luggage."

Caleb was staring at April as if mesmerized.

"Caleb?" his father repeated.

"Oh! Yes. Sure!"

Loren helped him unload the luggage from the cruiser and stack it onto the cart attached to the tractor that was their only means of transportation on the island.

"Coming with us?" Angus asked as the others climbed aboard.

"No, thanks," Loren answered. "I've got to get back to the house. Promised Dad I'd weed the garden before supper. Usual time for the mussel bake, Caleb?"

"Sure thing," Caleb answered.

The tractor roared into life and began the slow

climb up the hill. April was perched on one of the suitcases, hanging grimly onto the side of the cart. Loren turned and cut across along the cliffs towards his own house.

Loren shucked his boots at the kitchen door and dumped his mussels in the sink, ready for washing. The radio was muttering away in the corner. From the study down the hall his father's voice called out.

"That you, Loren? Grab a pencil, will you, and make a note of the tide times. They should be coming on."

Loren picked up the pencil and pad of paper that were kept by the radio. Still half-distracted, he turned up the volume and automatically noted the high tide and low tide times as the announcer gave them. Then the weather forecast brought his attention back sharply. Winds from the southeast and gusting to about forty knots. Possible rain by morning. They were in for a blow, that was certain.

It was almost dark by the time he slipped out of the house and made his way up the path to the treehouse. The wind was still rising. He and Caleb had built the house bit by bit during the past four years. What had started out as a basic shelter was now very sophisticated. High in the branches of one of the tallest spruces, it looked out over the island on one side, the sea on the other. The windows had glass panes; there was even a skylight. A narrow porch ran across the front of the main construction, which consisted of two rooms: their living room, complete with old couch, and the kitchen. Getting the couch up there had been a problem, which Caleb had solved by the simple expedient of ripping the whole living room floor out, hoisting the old bedspring and mattress up with the aid of an intricate series of pulleys, then replacing the floor. Not for nothing was it Caleb's ambition to be an engineer. A sturdy hanging ladder led up to the house.

Loren scrambled up the ladder, pulling it in after him out of habit. There were no other young people on the island now, but still, this was their private place. Caleb was here already; he could tell by the smoke coming from the chimney. Their tin-can stove would be ready for the mussels. He pulled open the door, crouched, and stepped inside. He was a lot taller now than when they had planned that door. He pulled it shut behind him.

Be interesting to hear what Caleb has to say about the new people, Loren thought, smiling in anticipation. Caleb had a gift for expressing himself. Caleb's bucket of mussels sat beside the stove. With what Loren had brought, they weren't going to go hungry!

"Caleb...," he began, then stopped dead. Caleb was sitting on a pillow on the floor, leaning comfortably against the wall. He was staring up at something with a totally foolish look on his face.

There, curled up in a corner of the couch, was April. Loren looked at her incredulously. Dressed the same as when he had last seen her, same useless shoes — how had she ever made it up the ladder?

"This is something else! I mean...it's *unreal!*" She was smiling.

Chapter 2

"W<small>HEN</small> C<small>ALEB</small> <small>TOLD</small> me you guys had a treehouse it nearly freaked me out. I mean, a *real* treehouse? Outside? I've never even seen one except in old movies. Like, for me the outdoors is the space between two boutiques, right?"

Loren glared at Caleb, speechless with fury. Caleb just shrugged and raised his eyebrows sheepishly.

"Hey." April looked from Loren to Caleb, then back to Loren. "Are you mad or something?"

Loren still couldn't speak.

"Look—I mean, when Caleb told his mom he was coming out to meet you at your treehouse I just asked...I mean, I just thought at least there's *something* interesting on this island and I wanted to come and see what it looked like. I didn't think you'd mind..."

"It's okay," Caleb said quickly. "It's just that Loren and me...well, it's been sort of our own place..." His words trailed off.

"*Sort* of our own place!" Loren turned to glare just as angrily at April. "No one has ever come up here except us. No one!"

April leaped up from the couch. The smile disappeared and her face turned as stormy as Loren's. "Well, excuse *me!* I didn't mean to barge in on your *private* place!" She headed for the door.

"Where are you going?" Caleb, too, jumped up.

"Back to your house. Where do you think? Heaven forbid I should barge in!"

Caleb reached out an arm to stop her. "Look, I'm sure it'll be all right, won't it, Loren?" He looked at Loren appealingly. "Come on, Loren, don't be owly."

Loren just kept glowering, his lips tightly shut.

"Forget it. I don't care." April twisted away from Caleb's restraining arm and pushed past Loren through the door. Seconds later they heard the rattle of the ladder being thrown furiously over the side. Caleb made as if to go after her, then stopped. Every freckle on his normally good-natured face stood out. He rubbed angrily at his close-cropped hair.

"You're some rude, Loren!" he exploded. "I guess I've got a right to invite somebody up here if I want!"

"Not without asking me, you don't," Loren raged back. "This is our treehouse. Nobody else's. We agreed it was to be private, remember? Always. We didn't even let David or Walt or anybody in when they were home for the holidays."

"She asked me. What was I supposed to say?"

"You were supposed to say no!"

"But she's a stranger. A visitor."

"All the more reason."

"I couldn't be rude. It doesn't come as easy to me as it does to you."

Loren threw down the bucket of mussels he had carried up. He could feel something exploding inside him. "Well, if that's the way it is then I don't have to worry any more!"

"Worry about what?" Caleb was almost shouting.

"Worry about *you,* that's what," Loren yelled back. "About leaving you to go off to school alone next fall. Because I'm not going!"

"You're *what?*" In his astonishment, Caleb's voice suddenly dropped back to normal.

"I'm not going! Not going to school on the mainland next fall. I'm staying here." The words were loud and defiant, but even as he spoke them, Loren could feel all the anger draining out of him and a sick, empty feeling take its place. This wasn't the way he had wanted to break the news. Not this way at all.

"Not going to school?" Caleb repeated, stunned. "Have you gone foolish? You've *got* to!"

"No, I don't."

"But you've got to go to school."

"I'll take correspondence courses. I've already written to the Ministry of Education. I can keep on here on my own for at least a couple of years — maybe right up until the end of high school."

"But why?" Caleb let himself fall back down onto the couch. "David, Pete, Walt — all the kids have gone. Why not you? There's nothing here for us now — you know that."

"Maybe not for you, not with the way the inshore fishing's going. But I'm not a fisherman's son." Loren half turned away and drew a deep breath. He controlled his voice with an effort. "I'm the lightkeeper's son. And the lighthouse is still here."

"But it doesn't need much tending any more," Caleb argued. "It'll be automated within a few years

— your dad says so himself. They'd never appoint you assistant keeper now. There's no need."

"Randalls have kept this light for over a hundred years, and I'm not going to leave."

"You have gone foolish. Plain foolish. You got the best marks of any of us at school, and now you're saying you're not going on." Caleb stopped to draw a breath as well. "And what about all our plans?" he went on. "What about rooming together at Mrs. Corkum's? It's bad enough having to leave the island, but I thought we'd at least go together!"

Loren didn't answer.

"What about your dad? He'll have something to say, I'm sure."

"I...I haven't told him yet."

Caleb sighed and shrugged. "There you are, then. He'll not listen to such nonsense. He'll make you go."

"Nobody can make me go. Nobody can *make* me do anything!"

"Good enough. You're right there, I suppose." Caleb got up and walked over to the buckets. He reached down and absent-mindedly began placing mussels on the grill over the smoking stove. His normal colour had returned, but his hands were shaking. "Still. You've got the summer to think it over. Maybe when the fall comes you'll change your mind."

"I won't, though," Loren said. He sounded mulish, even to his own ears. His hands were shaking even more than Caleb's and he dug them deep into his jacket pockets.

They roasted and ate the mussels in silence, cutting off chunks of the home-baked bread that Caleb had brought and slathering them in butter. They had cold milk to wash it all down with, but neither of them tasted what they ate. When they finished, Caleb doused the smouldering sticks in the can with water from the pail they kept beside it. Then he dumped the sticks into the empty mussel bucket. He lifted up the wire mesh in the bottom of the can that served as a grate, and dumped the ashes into that mussel pail as well. The other pail held more than a few leftover mussels — the first time *that* had ever happened. He and Loren tidied up, still without speaking more than absolutely necessary. Finally they picked up their buckets, went out onto the platform, pulled the door shut behind them, fastened it, and climbed down the ladder.

At the bottom Caleb seemed about to say something, then shrugged. "See you tomorrow, Loren."

"See you," Loren answered. They could have walked part of the way back together — usually did — but tonight each headed his own way without a word.

By morning the wind was shrieking across the island. When Loren came down to breakfast his father was already at the kitchen table, listening to the weather forecast.

"Looks like we're in for a good blow," he remarked mildly to Loren. "Dan Lohnes and his daughter aren't going to have too great a welcome back to the island." If he had noticed his son's angry entrance the night before, or his equally gloomy face this morning, he didn't mention it.

"Pity," Loren answered, going to the refrigerator for milk. He sat down opposite his father.

"Good mussel bake last night? Lucky the wind didn't come up so strong any sooner, wasn't it?"

"Um." Loren poured cereal into his bowl and reached for the sugar.

His father quirked an eyebrow at him. "I've got some work to do this morning — think you can manage dinner for us today? Angus called to say they got some cod in the seines yesterday. A chowder would go nicely. You could throw in some of that leftover lobster from the freezer."

For years now, Loren and his father had been on their own. Loren's mother had died when he was quite small and his four older brothers were all on the mainland, either working or at university. Breakfast and suppers were catch-as-catch-can affairs, but at noon one or the other of them produced a full, hearty meal. Lately Loren had been taking over more and more of the cooking. He had even begun baking bread, and Caleb's mother had pronounced it every bit as good as her own.

A chowder would mean going down to Caleb's house for the cod, but it couldn't be helped. He stretched the business of cleaning up the kitchen as long as he could, then reluctantly reached for his slicker and shoved his feet into his boots. As soon as he went out the kitchen door the wind hit him. The rain drove into his face. For a moment he staggered against their combined fury; then he leaned into it

23

and set off down the path to the wharf. With the weather this dirty, the men wouldn't have gone out fishing, he knew. Luckily Greg Winters had left with the cabin cruiser yesterday well before the storm struck.

As Loren forged his way towards the old wooden storehouse, he could see the four Cape Island fishing boats battened down securely on the slipways, and his father's dory bobbing in the dock. The water was roiling and slapping against it and sloshing over the wharf. The waves reached halfway up the slips. The harbour was small and not sheltered enough for all the boats to moor there safely, especially in storms like this one, so these Cape Islanders had flat-bottomed keels allowing them to be hauled well up out of the water each day. It was a good arrangement, although it meant that the men had to watch the tides carefully. The boats could not be brought up or launched at low tide. The Randalls' old Lunenburg dory was sturdy enough to take much worse seas than this, but Loren checked to make sure the lines were secure.

From inside the fish storehouse came sounds of hammering and voices. The men would be making use of their day off to repair traps and nets — fix up any things that needed doing on the boats. As Loren poked his head in, Caleb's father caught sight of him.

"You'll be wanting that cod. Just slip up to the house and Mother will give it to you. Caleb's up there as well with our young visitor. She and Dan are staying with us until they can get the house in shape to live in. You'll be wanting to see them, I'm sure."

Not really, Loren thought, but he headed back up

the path to Caleb's house. He knocked, then pushed open the back door and stepped into an enclosed porch. He shook off as much water as he could, tossed his slicker onto a hook, and kicked off his boots. In the kitchen he stopped in amazement. April was standing by the stove. Her cheeks were flushed, her hair was sticking out in untidy tufts, and there was a smudge of flour on her carefully made-up face. She was enveloped in one of Aunt Annie's voluminous aprons. Loren had always half-believed Aunt Annie could perform miracles; now he was sure of it.

"Can you believe it?" April announced proudly. "I'm baking bread!" Then, as she realized it was Loren, not Caleb, who had come in, her smile froze and she turned quickly away.

At that moment Caleb did walk in. He paused uncertainly when he saw Loren. Aunt Annie bustled through the dining room door. Caleb's mother wasn't really Loren's aunt, of course, but there were only five families left on the island now, all of them Landrys or Parkers, aside from Loren and his father, and the elders were "aunt" and "uncle" to all the young people.

"Loren!" she exclaimed. "I've got the cod all ready for you. Let me just get this bread in the oven. April, my dear, pop that pan in on the top rack and I'll put this in below."

For the first time in his life Loren felt awkward in Caleb's house — almost as if he, not April, were the stranger. He and Caleb avoided looking at each other. Before Loren could get the fish and leave, they heard the back door open and close. A moment later Dan Lohnes came in, shaking water from his hair. He slumped into the rocking-chair by the stove.

"You were right, Annie," he said, "the house is a mess."

"I'll just bet it is." April slammed the oven door. The sulky, closed look was back on her face.

"I'm sorry I couldn't do anything about getting it ready for you, Dan," Annie said, "but you didn't give me any time. If you'd let me know earlier…"

"I know. I made up my mind in such a hurry…maybe it was just a stupid idea."

"Oh, come on now, Dan," Annie said briskly. "The electricity's on, and the house is sound enough — it just needs a good scrubbing."

April raised her eyes to the ceiling and flung down the tea-towel she was holding. "Great. My friends are going to Florida for the summer — I get to scrub a filthy old house!"

"You wouldn't have been going to Florida with them anyway April. You know that," her father answered, stiffening in his chair and glaring at her. "We've been all through this!"

April glared back.

"She's been running with a wild bunch of kids," Dan said to Annie. "Too much money and too little to do. It'll do her good to spend a summer away from them."

April's mouth tightened. She whirled around and ran out through the hall door. Seconds later her feet could be heard pounding up the stairs.

"We'll help with the house, Dan," Annie said into the silence. "And you're both welcome to stay here as long as you want. Stay all summer, if you like, and forget about moving into the house at all. We've

plenty of spare room since Amy and the boys left."
She tucked a stray strand of hair behind her ear. There
was a warmth and comfort about her that immediately restored calm.

"Thanks, but no. I think we should be on our own.
I need time to myself." The rain lashed at the house.
"Melody's death has undone me, Annie." He stared,
unseeing, at the streaming windows. "I've tried, these
past months, but nothing did any good. And then,
all I could think of was to come here. Back to the
island."

"Back home," Annie said softly.

"I don't know," Dan answered, shoulders sagging
again. "I don't think I know where home is anymore."

Chapter 3

Loren lay for a long time that night, unable to sleep. The rain had let up, but the wind had shifted to the southwest, bringing in the fog. The regular, throbbing moan of the foghorn, which had been with him all his life and which, when he noticed it at all, usually soothed and reassured him, was no solace. The light was close enough and the fog thin enough up here that the beam could break through it and flash regularly in through his window. Three flashes and a pause. Three flashes and a pause. Its rhythm was part of Loren's very self, but tonight it, too, failed to comfort him. Troubled and guilty, he thought of Caleb. They had never had a real argument before. And his not going to school on the mainland was the last thing he had intended to fight over. He had agonized for days about the best way to tell Caleb — how had he let himself blurt it out so badly? It was Caleb's fault. Bringing April up to the treehouse. If anyone had betrayed anyone, it was Caleb. Loren rolled over and punched his pillow angrily. Of course it was Caleb's fault. He punched the pillow again and pulled it over his ears. All that did was block out the foghorn and the light. His thoughts still ran around.

The next morning he was up early, even before his father. The fog was hanging heavily over the garden as he slipped on his boots and slicker. Walking up the hill towards the lighthouse, he could hear the breathy hiss of air that preceded each blast of the foghorn. As he drew nearer, the noise became almost deafening. In the olden days, when his father and mother had lived in the small house attached to the light, the foghorn had to be operated manually. Someone had to be at the lighthouse continuously during foggy weather, ready to send out signals and answer any ship that called in with its own raspy horn. Nowadays, of course, the foghorn took care of itself. The little wooden building that had once been his parents' home now housed banks of gleaming electronic equipment. In addition to operating and monitoring the light, this equipment also sensed when the moisture in the air reached a certain level and automatically activated the horn. Far more efficient. Far safer. But Loren couldn't help thinking of his mother or father, sitting in the cold and damp, sometimes for hours, ready to answer a needy ship. And when they did, the ship's captain knew there was a human being there. Not just a machine, but a living person helping and guiding him, praying him in to safety.

Loren walked up past the lighthouse to the slate cliffs, but the fog blocked his view of the islands to the west. He stood there on the cliff edge for a moment, anyway. He liked the feel of the summer fog coming in off the sea. Then he continued along the cliffs, following a narrow path just outside the trees and bushes that grew along the cliff edges.

He passed Mussel Cove and cut inland to avoid the Breakages. The dead forest created an almost impenetrable barrier of bleached, silvery-grey drift-wood trees whose skeleton branches reached out to snare the unwary with spiky fingers. Skirting the edge of Low Swamp and the saltwater pond that had been open water when he was younger, he climbed back up to the easternmost part of the island. His father owned this piece of land as well as the lot their house stood on, and on all the island this was Loren's fa-vourite place. A thick stand of spruce and fir trees grew almost to the cliff's edge, but along the top of the cliffs was a mat of cranberry bushes. With the wall of trees behind him, he threw himself down onto this soft, springy carpet.

The fog was slowly dissipating, retreating over the ocean, and the sun was fitfully fighting its way clear. Patches of warm sunlight vied with the woolly white dampness. Gradually, the wet cranberry mat dried to a soft, fragrant, sun-warmed bed, and the air was rich with an earthy, tangy, spruce-tinged smell. The sound of a bell buoy drifted over to him, but there was nothing to be seen but the surging waves, with the fetch of hundreds of miles of ocean behind them. He watched the breakers crashing onto the rocks below him.

"Seas come in threes," the fishermen steadfastly maintained in the face of all the scientific theories the island schoolteachers could throw at them. Loren counted. Three huge waves, then a series of lesser ones. Then three big ones again. Or was it just his imagination? He wasn't sure, but he tended to side with the fishermen anyway. Scientific theories were fine in classrooms, but Caleb's father and the other island men spent their lives on the sea, and who should know it, after all, better than they?

Reluctantly, Loren got up and dusted himself off. It was time to be getting back. There was work to be done around the house and garden, and his father was too frail to be doing much of it himself. If Loren went away, who would help him? Loren shrugged irritably. He would cut through the swamp on his way home. There was a heron's nest he had been watching — last week there had been four hatchlings in it. He was annoyed that he hadn't brought his field glasses. They were so much a part of him it was unlike him to forget them.

The heron's nest was high up in a tall, dead tree, almost in the middle of the swamp. Blue eggshells littered the ground underneath it. The trunk and its exposed roots were whitened with excrement. The tree was too fragile to support a climber, but another fallen trunk angled high enough beside it that Loren could climb it and look in without getting too close. He shucked off his boots and climbed carefully in his socks, toes gripping for holds on the splintery wood. The nest was an untidy, prickly collection of twigs and small sticks. Loren kept his eyes on it as he got closer, moving as slowly and as quietly as he could. In spite of his caution, however, the mother heron suddenly lumbered up and with a hoarse "gronk" lurched over to a nearby branch. She stared at Loren resentfully. He froze until, with another loud protest, the heron took off over the trees. It was hard to believe that such an ungainly, bulky bird could look so graceful in flight.

There was only one chick left. Dark grey, scruffy, awkward-looking, it was so big that it was practically stuffed into the nest. Nevertheless it surveyed Loren and the motherless world around it with terrified squeaks. Loren made a note on the pad he always carried with him, then clambered back down. Reluctant or not, the chick would probably be gone by the next time he came.

Old Grampus sparkled now in the sunlight as he retraced his steps to the lighthouse. The water over the shoal was a paler, lighter green than the seas around it, and the whitecaps were breaking over it. The Groaner groaned faithfully with every tossing wave.

As Loren pushed into the kitchen he heard voices. There, sitting at the kitchen table talking to his father, was April. She sprang up as he came in, a wary look on her face.

"Caleb's mom sent me over with a pie. Caleb went out fishing early this morning with the men." She hesitated, then went on quickly. "She says you can bake it yourself — it's ready for the oven. Just put it in at 450 for ten minutes, then down to 350 for about thirty or forty minutes. She said you know enough about pies to judge when it's done...which is more than I do!" She laughed nervously.

Unexpected things always threw Loren, and this was certainly unexpected.

"April and I have been exchanging stories," Loren's father put in. "She's been telling me about the big city, and I've been telling her about the island. You'll have to show her around a bit, Loren."

She'd just love that, Loren thought sourly.

"I've had my breakfast," his father continued. "I've a report that has to go out to the Department of Transport today when the boats go over to the mainland, so I'll get to work. Stay and have a cup of tea with Loren here, April. He's the one can really tell you about the island. Knows every stick and stone on the place, and every animal and bird to boot." He pushed back his chair and, leaning on the table to take the weight off his bad hip, slowly got to his feet. Loren held out a hand to help and gave him his cane.

After he left Loren and April eyed each other like two strange dogs.

"I guess you don't want me around," April finally said. "I've got to get back, anyway." She grimaced. "Help Dad with that horrible house."

"No, wait." Loren spoke quickly, then wished he hadn't. He would really rather that she go. It was too late now, though. Besides, he was feeling guilty about the other night. He had been rude. He should apologize.

He walked over to the stove, where the kettle was steaming as usual. The stove was like most of the others on the island: electric, with an electric oven, but with a side part that burned wood and kept the iron plate on top of it constantly warm. There were only a few days in the middle of the summer when the extra warmth wasn't appreciated.

"Would you like a cup of tea?" he asked.

April was on her way to the door. "No, thanks. I'd really better get back." Her face was blank, her tone cold.

Now Loren was perversely determined that she should stay. If he was going to apologize, she should at least be polite enough to listen. "I'm sorry about the other night...," " he began.

"That's okay. I don't care. Really. Forget it."

Loren was beginning to get mad all over again. "I *am* sorry," he repeated. "I was just surprised to see you there, that's all."

"It's okay. I won't go back. Don't worry. Look, I've *really* got to go." Without another word she was out the door and gone.

Loren looked after her, fuming.

He had just poured himself some tea when there was a hesitant knock on the door and April peeked back in. She looked decidedly uncomfortable. Loren couldn't be sure, but under all her make-up she might have been blushing. Her ears were red.

"I forgot. Mrs. Landry asked if I'd bring back that bowl she sent the cod up in yesterday. She needs it." Then, surprisingly, she broke out laughing. "Man, that blew my dignified exit, didn't it? You wouldn't believe it — I'm always doing things like that. I can't do anything right!" She was still laughing, but there was no laughter in her voice. It was angry. Almost fierce.

After she left, Loren drank his tea and scrambled two eggs. He rinsed the dishes, then headed out to the garden. With yesterday's rain and today's sun, the weeds would be thriving. When he finished the gardening he fed the chickens, collected the eggs, and mended the coop where a small hole had been letting the two most determined hens out to have free run of the garden. It was a job he'd been putting off for at least a week. When he finished that, he dragged the lawnmower out of the shed and attacked the already neat patch of grass that was their front lawn.

"Loren! Are you determined to work yourself silly all morning?" His father was standing on the porch and waving an envelope at him. "Will you take this down to Uncle Angus? He said he'd stop off for it when the men come back from the fishing grounds, before he went on to West Harbour."

Loren straightened up. Back to Caleb's? An excuse was on the tip of his tongue, but he knew the report had to go in, and the unnecessary walk would be hard on his father. Besides, he was used to dropping by Caleb's house once a day, if not more. How would he explain his sudden reluctance to go? Loren was certain that if his father knew all the facts he would be even less sympathetic.

His steps got slower as he neared the Landrys' door; he could only hope that April wouldn't be around. The men weren't in yet, he knew, so Caleb wouldn't be back. Maybe he could just leave the report with Aunt Annie and leave.

Aunt Annie was at the stove when he came in; April was nowhere to be seen. Loren heaved a sigh of relief. He had started to explain why he was there when the CB radio on the counter crackled to life.

"Just a minute, Loren, that must be Angus." Aunt Annie rushed over to answer with their own call numbers. "He's here, Angus. Yes, looks like he's got it." She raised her eyebrows questioningly at the envelope in Loren's hand, and he nodded back. "I'll call the trucks now," she went on. "Good enough!" She signed off. "They're on their way in. I'll just phone up the fish plant so the trucks will be out at West Harbour to meet them. Angus will stop by the island and pick up that report. Do you want to take it on down to the wharf? They're in early," she added. "Can't have had much luck." She shook her head, then headed for the telephone.

Loren looked all around again. Still no sign of April.

"Was there anything else you wanted, Loren?" Aunt Annie paused as she saw him standing there. "April's over at the house helping her father, if you wanted to see her."

"No...no...that's okay." Loren turned and made for the door, stumbling over the rocking-chair on the way. Now he'd have to face Caleb, after all.

Chapter 4

Angus Landry looked tired. He tossed a line to Loren. As the boat nosed in, Caleb jumped out and held the stern. Neither boy greeted the other.

"Are you in a hurry, Loren?" Angus asked. "Would you like to come to the harbour with us, then?"

Loren hesitated, but the sight of the trim Cape Islander straining at her line and the thought of the open seas were irresistible. "Sure. I'll help you unload."

"I'm glad to have you come, but we don't need much help, I'm sorry to say," Angus replied. "There were so few mackerel today it wasn't worth going out. Those draggers and seiners — they're breaking up the schools, breaking up the spawning grounds with their great nets tearing at the bottom." He sighed. "With all the modern equipment we've got nowadays, if the fish were there we'd be flourishing. But they're just not there." He straightened up painfully and flexed his arms to relieve the aching muscles. "Except for the herring of course. Shaking herring — that's a thankless job. The seine was mashed all full of *them*."

Loren had been out in the boat often enough to know what a tiresome, heavy ordeal it was to clear the seines of the small herring that got caught in the mesh. The net had to be hauled up, a bit at a time, and all the trapped herring shaken out. Only after they were all out could the nets be pursed and the mackerel taken into the boats.

They cast off and headed out of the harbour towards the mainland. Caleb and Loren balanced themselves against the gunnels in the stern where the fish boxes were, just aft of the small forward cabin where Angus stood to steer. The boat rose and fell easily in the light seas. The six-cylinder engine was so noisy that conversation was almost impossible. Loren relaxed, and watched as the island dropped behind them. Long after the houses had disappeared from view he could still see the red and white column of the lighthouse. This was his home. This place and no other. How could he leave?

The trucks were waiting at the wharf and the work of unloading the fish from the other boats was well under way. Angus was right. It didn't take much time to unload their boxes.

"I'll just walk on up to the store and mail your father's report, Loren," Angus said when they had finished. "Anything else you need there?"

"No, thanks. We were into town for supplies just last week."

"Good enough. Be back in a while."

Loren and Caleb stretched out on the wharf facing the sun, backs against a stack of lobster pots. Loren picked at a frayed rope nervously. It was queer, this. There'd never been a moment of uneasiness between them before.

Finally, Caleb broke the silence. "Are you still determined, then, not to go to the mainland to school?"

"Yes."

"You make me feel so guilty, you!" The words came out in a furious burst of anger.

Loren looked up in shocked surprise. "What...what do you mean?"

Caleb, normally so unperturbable, jumped to his feet and towered over Loren. "*I* should be the one staying, not you! If one of us ever had a good reason to stay it would be me!"

"What do you mean?" Loren repeated incredulously. "Why in the world should you stay?"

"You saw him today!" Caleb exploded. "Every day it gets harder and harder for him. He's not young anymore. I'm the last of my father's sons. What will he do when I'm gone and he's alone? How much longer will he be able to fish?"

"But there's no room for you on the boats," Loren protested. "Uncle Angus has said so himself. There's not enough fish now even for the men who are still at it. He doesn't *want* you to stay, any more than he wanted Pete or David to stay."

"Your father doesn't want you to stay, either. There's no work for you at all. And yet you're bound *you'll* stay!"

"My father's older. And he's alone. What would he do without me?" Loren countered. "Anyway," he went on. "You want to be an engineer. You know it yourself, Caleb. You've never wanted to be a fisherman."

"I know." Caleb's anger deserted him as suddenly

as it had struck. "I know," he repeated. "That's why I feel so guilty. I *don't* want to stay. But none of the others did. *I* should..."

"Hey, there!" A loud voice startled them. They turned to see a heavy-set man in a windbreaker bearing down on them. "You boys from Windward Island?"

"Yes," Caleb called back.

Loren's mouth tightened as the man strode up to them. He was a real-estate agent who had been nosing around the island the month before. Rumour had it that he had already bought up two abandoned houses and was sniffing around for more. The last thing they needed was for a bunch of strangers to move in.

"Could I get a ride over to the island with you boys, do you think?" the man called out heartily. "My name's McIvor."

"Sure..." Caleb started to answer.

"The men won't be coming back to the mainland again today," Loren interrupted quickly. "You wouldn't be able to get back."

"No problem. I've got a friend can pick me up later on."

Just then Angus appeared, and the real-estate agent turned to greet him. "I've been asking the boys here if you could give me a ride over to the island. Got some business to talk over with you folks."

"Don't see why not," Angus answered good-naturedly. "Hop aboard. Cast off the lines there, boys, and we'll be on our way."

When they reached the island, Angus dispatched Caleb to round up all the islanders. Mr. McIvor had asked for a general meeting at Angus's house. Loren strode up to his own house and slammed in through the kitchen door angrily.

"Whoa, there. What's biting you?" His father looked up from the kitchen table, surprised.

"That real-estate agent's here. You know, the one that was here last month. He's at Uncle Angus's. Wants to talk to everybody."

"Does he now?" His father got up stiffly. "That's interesting. Hand me my cane, Loren. We'll just be off to see what he's got in mind."

"You're not going?" Loren burst out.

"Of course I am. Why ever wouldn't I?"

"But we're not interested in selling. We won't ever be. Why would you want to see him?"

"If anything's going on, I want to know about it." He took the cane that Loren held out to him and made for the peg on the wall where his jacket hung. "Besides, you never know. It might be worth our while to hear what he has to say."

Loren started to protest further, but his father ignored him and went on out through the door.

By the time they reached the Landrys' house, all the other islanders were gathered, except for Dan Lohnes.

"I couldn't find Dad," April was explaining a little breathlessly to Caleb, as they seated themselves side by side on the piano bench in the living room. "He spends a lot of time just wandering around by him-self — I don't know where he's gone this morning. I thought I'd come anyway. Anything to get away from

41

that revolting house. Maybe I can sell *it* to this guy."
She laughed.

The living room was full, and some people had
spilled over into the dining room and were perched
on chairs around the table. Uncle Lem and Auntie
Pearl, as the island's oldest residents, had been given
the seat of honour on the couch.

"William!" Angus called as Loren and his father
came in. "We've saved a seat for you." He helped
Loren's father to a chair beside the couch. Loren
remained standing in the doorway, staring resentfully
at Mr. McIvor.

The real-estate agent cleared his throat, coughed,
and began.

"Well, now," he said. "I expect some of you have
heard that my company has bought up those two
empty houses back of the pond there, and I guess
you're wondering why. Well, I'll tell you." He seemed
to be warming up and gradually becoming more at
ease. "You folks here are sitting on a lovely piece of
property. I mean, a *lovely* piece of property." He
paused to let his words sink in.

"We know," old Frank Parker said tersely. "Get on
with it, then."

A little disconcerted, the real-estate agent hurried
on. "The fact is," he said, "my company is interested
in buying more property here. In fact...my company
is interested in buying *all* the property here."

There was a general rustle. "Seems to be one problem with that, Mr. McIvor," Angus remarked. "We
live here."

The real-estate agent pounced, his assurance restored. "That's right, Mr. Landry. Of course, that's

42

right! But I've taken the liberty of checking some facts, and it seems to me that with the fishing doing as poorly as it is, and getting worse all the time, it's not going to be very long before you'll all be forced to sell and move to the mainland. If I may speak plainly, I know that your incomes depend entirely on the fishing, and they're dropping every year. I'm offering you a chance to sell before you get desperate, and I'm offering you top prices for your homes. You can check it yourselves on the mainland. I'm not here to cheat you — I'm here to offer you the best deal you'll ever have!"

There was silence for a moment; then William Randall spoke. "Why? Why, Mr. McIvor, is your company so interested in our island?"

"Why?" the real-estate agent echoed. "I'll tell you honestly. Because this island could be a goldmine for us. You'll see I'm not trying to put anything over on you at all. People from the mainland, even people from the States, are just clamouring for vacation spots like this. With a little fixing up, a little tidying here and there, we'd make a packet on the real estate here, my company and you folks, too."

"No way!" Loren sprang to his feet. Caleb and April looked at him, startled. His father sent him a warning look. Loren didn't see it, wouldn't have cared if he had. "This is our home! We don't want it 'fixed up' or 'tidied,' and we don't want strangers here!"

"You'll not get *my* house!" Uncle Lem heaved himself up from the couch and glared. "Come on, Mother, I'll not stay and listen t'another word o' this nonsense!" Practically dragging Auntie Pearl, he stomped furiously out of the room. The whole house

43

shook as he slammed the door on the way out.

Uncle Lem's son, Clarence, made a move to go after his father, then sat back down, rubbing at his forehead with a shaky hand. "Father's a bit brisk," he apologized. "A little set in his ways." He looked nervously at his wife, Vera. "I think I'd like to hear a piece more about this. I've lost money this year, and while he won't admit it, Father's done the same. I'd like to hear more; wouldn't you, Mother?" His wife nodded nervously.

"*Well* then, let me tell you..." The real-estate agent launched into figures, deals, interest rates, and mortgages. No one noticed as Loren turned and almost ran out the back door.

His house seemed strangely empty, but comforting and familiar. Loren couldn't imagine living anywhere else. *We'll* never sell, he thought mutinously. *My* father's income doesn't depend on the fishing. And Uncle Lem will never sell. Windward Island turned into a tourist resort? Impossible! Yet he couldn't quite quieten the fear that had settled in the pit of his stomach.

The next morning at breakfast, neither Loren nor his father brought up the subject of Mr. McIvor. Loren escaped as soon as he could, and occupied himself with chores until dinnertime at noon. Even then he ate as quickly as he could, dreading that his father might mention the real-estate agent. It was almost as if just talking about it might make it happen. As soon as dinner was over, he went up to his room and pulled the door shut behind him. Absent-mindedly, he sat down at his desk and picked up a smooth block of cedar. He ran his fingers over it, gradually paying more attention to it. It was a particularly nice piece.

Loren looked around. On the shelves built into the four walls of his room birds perched. Barn swallows hovered, poised in swift flight. Robins, juncos, brightly hued warblers: nearly every bird that Loren had ever seen on the island was represented here. On the wall by the door his first, clumsy attempts; the later birds in the light by the window more delicate, detailed — his skill making them so real they seemed to move even as he watched them. In the corner, suspended by fine wires from the ceiling, a seagull soared on an imaginary air current, wings outstretched to the fullest.

Loren picked up a knife, tested the blade against his thumb, and stared at the cedar. Mostly, he found his wood on the island here — fir and spruce, sometimes driftwood picked up from the beach for perches and background. This piece had been sent by his brother Walt, who was studying forestry at the University of New Brunswick.

A loud knock on his door much later that afternoon startled him. He had been so engrossed he had lost track of the time. As usual, he thought ruefully. The lumpish, awkward shape of a baby heron sprawled in a prickly nest was just beginning to take form in the cedar. Loren sat back and shrugged his shoulders, loosening the muscles. Amazing, he thought. It's almost harder to make something ugly than to make something beautiful. But he couldn't really believe the young heron to be ugly. There was life and the promise of power to come in that clumsy shape. Loren was satisfied.

"Come in," he called.

"Loren!"

His father's voice was angry. This was so unusual that Loren looked up, startled.

"I've just been to Angus for tea. Caleb told me something I can't believe."

"What did he tell you?" But, with a sinking feeling, Loren already knew.

His father pushed his way into the room, hardly favouring his bad leg. He gave an impatient tap on the floor with his cane.

"He says you've decided not to go to school on the mainland next fall. Says you've got it all worked out that you'll stay here and take correspondence courses, or some fool thing."

"It's not a 'fool thing.'" Loren rose to face his father. "Lots of people take correspondence courses."

"Then it's true?"

"Yes. It's true. I hate it on the mainland. You know that. Even when we have to go over to buy supplies. It's so hot and noisy — so many people everywhere. I can't live there, Dad. You must know that!"

His father shrugged impatiently. "I know you have no choice. What would you do here?"

"I can study...we don't know for sure that they wouldn't appoint me assistant keeper when I'm older. Randalls have kept this light for over a hundred years!"

William Randall made a slight grimace and reached out for the back of Loren's chair. Stiffly, he eased himself into it. He sighed. "That real-estate fellow

46

was right, you know." He raised his hand as Loren began to protest. "I know you don't want to talk about it, but not talking about a problem won't make it go away. Things change, Loren. And things are changing on this island, whether you like it or not. There'll be no job for you here. All the lights on this coast will be fully automated within a few years, including this one. I don't like it any more than you do, son, but that's just the way it is."

"They've been saying that since 1971 and it hasn't happened yet." Loren faced his father almost desperately. "The fishermen don't trust machines without men behind them to keep them working properly, and they're right. What would happen if something went wrong with the light and you weren't here? It might be days before they even found out about it, let alone got someone out here to fix it. What would happen in the meantime?"

"You're exaggerating, Loren. With all the back-up systems it's not likely anything will go wrong, and if it did, it wouldn't take that long to fix it." He stopped for a moment, then looked past Loren out the window, up to the lighthouse. "In a few years there won't be any fishermen left around here, anyway." Now his voice just sounded tired. "No inshore fishermen in their own boats, that is. Just the big offshore trawlers and draggers with all their fancy equipment. That's the way it is," he repeated. "You've got to be sensible."

"I don't believe it," Loren insisted stubbornly. "I don't *believe* that's going to happen. And Caleb had no right to tell you what I'm going to do. *I* was going to tell you when I was ready."

"He thought I should know before it was too late, and I'm glad he did." His father caught Loren's eyes with his own and held them. "You've got to think this over a lot more carefully, Loren. Your brothers have all gone — look how well they're doing. You have to go, too."

"But what about you? What will you do when I'm gone?"

He stood up with an abrupt movement and stumbled slightly, then waved away Loren's instinctive move to help him. A trace of his original anger returned. "I can look after myself very nicely, thank you, for a good many years yet. I'm not incapable, you know," he said with more than a touch of asperity. "It's not on my account that you need be staying here."

Loren turned back to his desk. He picked up the just-begun carving and smoothed a rough spot with one finger. "It's not just that," he said, so quietly it could hardly be heard. "It's...it's...I really *don't* want to leave."

"We have to do many things we don't want to, Loren," his father answered. He waited a moment; when Loren didn't answer, he went on. "Think it over. That's all I'm asking you right now. Just think it over."

Loren didn't look up as his father left the room and closed the door behind him.

Loren stared at the carving. He picked up his knife, then tossed it back down. He walked over to the door, paused for a moment, and opened it. He could hear his father downstairs in the kitchen. He went on down and headed for the front door, stopping just long enough to call to him.

"I'm going over to clean the light."

"But you just cleaned it last..." The door closed, cutting him off.

Loren trudged up to the lighthouse. In the storeroom under the stairs he found cloths and polish. This storeroom had been his parents' bedroom. The modern lightkeeping equipment was in what had been their front parlour. Of the old kitchen there remained not a trace. He climbed up the three narrow flights of stairs, opened the trap door at the top, and stepped up into the light room. Glass windows on all sides afforded him an unobstructed view of the whole island and the sea around it. To the west, the Brother Islands. Farther to the south he could catch a glimpse of Out Island. People had never settled there. Once fishermen had built shacks that would house them for a night or two in the days when they rowed out to fish in dories and it was too far for them to get back to the mainland each evening. Those shacks had long since fallen down.

Loren switched the light off. It ground slowly to a halt. The light itself was a 400-watt mercury vapour lamp, with three lenses and one dead spot. This produced the three flashes and one pause. It ran on electricity now, and had for twenty years, but before that it had been powered by huge springs that had had to be wound with a crank. Loren had often heard his father tell of how, on one bitterly cold night, a spring had broken and his mother had had to turn the light by hand until his father and his assistant had been able to get it fixed. There had been oil lamps with wicks that had needed trimming, too, in those days, smoky lenses that had needed cleaning, and metal reflectors that had needed polishing. The lenses still needed polishing, of course, but the job was much easier now. The most work, and the work Loren enjoyed the most, was polishing the brass frames that held the lenses in place. They were bright and untarnished, but he set to it, anyway.

Within half an hour he was finished. The sun was just beginning to set over the Brother Islands. He turned the light back on, then stood in front of one of the huge windows and watched as the dusk gradually took over the sea and the land alike. With one last defiant splash of red and gold, the sun finally sank between Big and Little Brother; then there was darkness, and only Loren's own sombre reflection staring back at him from the glass.

Chapter 5

Loren stayed as close to home as possible for the next few days. Caleb was out fishing with the men every day, so he managed to avoid him. He did see April once, however, when he passed the old Lohnes' house on his way down to the wharf on an errand. She had hung a rug over the washing line in the back yard and was whacking it with an old-fashioned rug beater. Loren made no attempt to attract her attention. Even if he had wanted to, the grim look on her face and the furious way she was attacking the rug were warnings-off enough. He saw Dan Lohnes a couple of times, but only from a distance. April's father had taken to walking on the cliffs beyond the lighthouse in the late afternoons, but his dejected, lonely-looking figure did not invite company.

Loren worked in the garden and around the house, and finished the baby heron, his best carving yet. He and his father went on as before, but there was a difference. The old, easy familiarity was not quite there. They were too polite. Too careful. His father didn't bring the subject of school up again, but Loren could feel it there between them. Then word came that the real-estate company had bought another island house, one that old Frank's brother had lived in until he had retired to the mainland. The family had kept the house to come back to now and then, and Loren had never imagined that they would give it up. McIvor must have made them a pretty good offer. Loren's stomach knotted again at the thought of it. He threw himself into a frenzy of work.

He decided to paint the lighthouse. It had been done the spring before, and they were only committed to painting it every second year, but there was paint handy and Loren had to do something. He began the job on a bright sunny day and had it almost done within a week. Then one morning he awoke to all the signs of a gale. Dawn had broken fiery red, and the night before there had been a huge ring around the moon. "The bigger the ring, the nearer the wet," the old saying went. He had gone down to breakfast to find his father tapping the barometer thoughtfully.

"It's dropping fast," William Randall said. "Too fast. This is going to be a big one." He had turned the radio on, but the weather reports had not been broadcast yet. "I think you'd better go down and secure the dory, Loren. Pull it right up and lash it down. The moon's full and the tide will be full high, and with the wind that's getting up it will be even higher. Pull the dory right up to the top of the slipway."

By the time Loren got down to the wharf all the other men were there. They knew the signs too well to have gone out that morning. All four boats were up on the slipways and secured. Fish boxes, lobster pots, everything loose was being carried into the fish house.

"Loren! I'll help you with the dory." It was Caleb.

Loren was tempted to refuse, but decided that would be childish. Besides, hauling up the dory was too big a job for him alone.

"Thanks," he said shortly.

Together they dragged the boat well above the highest tide line they could imagine, then lashed it down. The wind was blowing fitfully by the time they finished, and the seas were beginning to roll in — heavy, ponderous swells that looked smooth and oily until they hit the breakwater at the harbour mouth and exploded into a fury of spray. Loren watched, mesmerized. As always it was an incredible sight — beautiful in its wildness, but forbidding and frightening in its power.

"We'd better get on home," Caleb jerked him back to reality. "There's a lot to be done there as well."

Loren took one last look along the sweep of the coast beyond the harbour. The gulls, instead of soaring and swooping far out over the waves, were feeding greedily along the coastline, side by side with dozens of raucous, bickering crows. The few birds that were in the air were heading inland, low over the fields and trees. They, too, knew that a storm was coming, and were stocking up and seeking shelter.

Loren followed Caleb past the old Parkers' house. Auntie Pearl at eighty-one and Uncle Lem at eighty-two were the only really old people left on the island.

Their son, Clarence, and his wife, no longer young themselves, lived in the house just behind and lent a hand when needed. They couldn't really be said to be taking care of their parents, though. Uncle Lem still went out in the boats more often than not, and Auntie Pearl had more energy than almost any other two people put together. She was on the back door-step now, a tiny, bird-like woman with the quick, pert movements of a sparrow, waving fiercely with a tea-towel at smoke that was billowing out the kitchen door.

"M'stove's smokin' t'beat the band! Wind's haulin' for certain!" she shouted as the boys hurried by. No electric stove for her. She still produced the best pies and bread on the island in an old-fashioned black wood-burner.

Loren and Caleb waved back and kept on up the path.

When they reached Caleb's house, they found Aunt Annie on the porch. "Have you boys seen April? Dan said she went out for a walk earlier on and hasn't come back yet. I don't know if she realizes what a storm's brewing."

"She wasn't down at the wharf," Caleb answered. "Maybe I'd better just go check along the shoreline. Loren, will you keep an eye out for her on your way?"

"Sure," Loren answered. He had a sudden picture of April in her city clothes and useless shoes scrambling along the cliffs in a storm. She couldn't be so stupid. Anyone could tell it was going to blow. He went on home, where his father was getting every-thing loose into the barn. They had kept cattle at one time, but with the shortage of pasture land on the island, the stores on the mainland, and refrigerators and freezers in the houses, the cattle had become more of a nuisance than a boon. They still had the chickens, however — and, sure enough, the two most determined hens had escaped the coop again despite his efforts.

By the time Loren had rounded them up the sun had disappeared and the wind was moaning ominously through the trees. The sea was now dark and choppy; white-crested combers raced in a wild, tumultuous charge to the shore. Loren remembered April, then dismissed the thought. She would surely be back at the house by now.

"Guess that's all we can do." The words were torn out of William Randall's mouth and blown away into the wind. "I said," he shouted again, cupping his hands around his mouth and yelling directly at Loren, "that's all we can do. Let's get back to the house."

Just then Loren remembered the lighthouse. He had opened the windows on the ground floor the day before to air out the smell of paint, and had left them open for the night. They would have to be closed now.

"The windows at the lighthouse are open," he shouted back. "I'll go and close them."

"Good enough." His father waved and made for the house.

Loren was halfway up to the lighthouse when the rain hit, driving in horizontally, transformed by the blowing wind into jagged slivers of ice-like needles. He began to run. His eyes on the treacherous and now-muddy path under his feet, he didn't even see the figure running towards him. The force of the collision almost knocked him over and he reached out more to keep his balance than to help. It took a moment to get his breath back; then he saw who was standing, panting, in front of him.

"April!"

Her hair was soaking wet and plastered against her head, streams of water ran in black, mascara-laden rivulets down her cheeks, and her clothes were clinging to her like wet rags. To Loren's total amazement, she was laughing.

"Man, isn't this something else!" she exclaimed.

He grabbed her hand and tugged her towards the lighthouse. "Come on, you idiot! Let's get inside!"

The windows were open and the shutters banging. Together Loren and April latched everything up securely. Only then did Loren think about dry clothes.

"There are some sweaters hanging in the storeroom here," he said, shaking his wet hair back out of his eyes. "I'll get a couple."

April was still laughing. She looked like a cat that had been left out all night in a hurricane. Loren instinctively looked at her feet. To his surprise she wore a sturdy, sensible pair of rubber boots.

She saw him looking at the boots. "Some change, isn't it? They belong to Amy — Caleb's sister. Lucky for me Aunt Annie made me put them on before I went out. Super cool, don't you think?" In the excitement of the storm, she seemed to have forgotten Loren's outburst in the treehouse.

Loren didn't know what to say. He hung his slicker on a hook behind the door, tossed her a grey wool fisherman's pullover, then took another one down for himself. "I'm going on up to the light," he got out, finally. "You can change here."

Without waiting for her to answer, he started to climb the stairs. It felt very much like running away, but he couldn't think of anything else to do. In a few seconds, however, her head popped up through the trap door behind him.

"Can I come up, too? I've never been up in a light-house before." She had to shout to make herself heard above the roaring of the wind and the rattling of the huge windows.

Loren gestured her in and leaned down to give her a hand. They stood for a moment, side by side. The small, round light room was an oasis of peace and warmth. Outside all was in lashing confusion. The sea had broached the wall marking the boundary of the saltwater pond and reclaimed it, at least for the time being. Waves were beating on both sides of the narrow strip of land that separated them from the swamp and the Breakages rising beyond. Now, as they watched, the surging waters met to battle in a tower-ing cascade of foaming spray. The island was cut in half.

Finally Loren became aware of the fact that they were both shivering in spite of the dry sweaters. There was an electric hotplate on a counter in the store-room, and some instant coffee. With a last look at the turmoil outside, he motioned to April to follow him and led the way back down the stairs.

The relative quiet of the shuttered storeroom shocked him for a moment. He switched on a light — at least the generators were doing their job — and plugged in the hotplate. As he handed April her mug she spoke.

"In the city, you know, when it rains, you just stay in or go to the movies or something." She looked at him. Even though she had made an effort to scrub off all the smudged make-up, her eyes still looked huge in her pale face. "Is it always like this here?"

"Not always. This is a pretty big storm." He paused, not knowing what to say next. His mind was still full of the frenzy outside the light room window. "The fishermen don't like the weather, of course, but I do. Big storms like this are..."

"Awesome." She gave the word its true meaning.

"You're not scared?"

"Oh, no! I love it!" Her coffee spilled over a bit as she took a gulp. "It's not like fog. I hate fog!"

"Why? I sort of like it."

"It frightens me."

"It fascinates me. It doesn't 'roll in' you know, the way it says in books. At least, not all the time. Sometimes if you stand at our kitchen window you can see it just sneaking in from the sea. In little bits that you'd think you could just blow away. Then suddenly you're all closed in."

April shuddered. "It's sneaky, all right."

Loren searched for something to say. "How's the house coming?" he asked lamely.

"Ugh."

"I saw your dad a couple of times. He walks out on the cliffs a lot."

"Yes." April's face hardened.

Loren went on, tentatively. "He looks really lonely..."

April slammed the coffee cup back down onto the counter. It missed the edge and crashed to the floor. "Of course he's lonely — my mother died, didn't she?"

"I'm sorry..." Loren began, shocked, but April didn't seem to hear him.

"She was his whole life. He was her whole life. They lived for each other. What's he supposed to do when his whole reason for being alive disappears?"

"But...but he's still got you..."

"Me? Why in the world would you think *that* would be important? What use would having *me* be to him? They had each other. They didn't need me then. He certainly doesn't need me now."

"But she was your mother. You must miss her, too."

"You're the only one who seems to have thought of that. You and Aunt Annie. With everyone else, it's 'Poor Dan, how will he ever get along without Melody? Poor Dan, he and Melody were so close.' "

"But surely...I mean — my dad and I are alone, too...surely the two of you could help each other..."

"That doesn't seem to have occurred to *him*."

"Maybe if you..."

"Look. He doesn't want me. It's okay." She shrugged, her face defiant. "I don't know why I even said all that. It's okay, really. I've always gotten along. I always will." She caught sight of the spilled coffee. "Oh, God! I've spilled the coffee *and* broken the cup. Where's a cloth or something? I'll clean it up."

"No — don't bother," Loren started to protest. "It doesn't matter. Look — isn't there anything..."

"No! I'm okay. I shouldn't have said anything and I don't want to talk about it anymore." She grabbed a roll of paper towels from the counter and mopped furiously at the mess.

Loren looked at her for a moment, about to say something more. Then he reached for the towels instead and knelt to help her.

Chapter 6

Two days later the skies were clear again, but the cove and the beach were strewn with bits of wood, corks, buoys — all sorts of debris. Stones as large as boulders had been carried in and dumped on the low-lying ground. The swamp was littered with smashed and dead trees.

As soon as Loren had a free moment he slung his field glasses around his neck and decided to have a look around. The young heron had long since left its nest, but there was a family of muskrats in the freshwater pond near the treehouse that had had kits just a few weeks ago. He should check on them.

He climbed to the top of the lighthouse for a quick survey. The island was whole again, and the saltwater pond was a pond again, but the wall between it and the sea had been greatly diminished. Idly, he wondered how long it would take for the ocean to build it back up, rock by rock, or whether another gale would tear it down entirely. Suddenly he caught sight of a single figure trudging far out by the low tide line. As he watched the solitary man, April's words came back to him. Lonely and lost Dan Lohnes might be, Loren thought, but he wasn't the only one.

The gulls were back out over the ocean again, swooping and calling ceaselessly. "Like mournful souls in pain." He'd read that somewhere in a book. A bit romantic, but pretty descriptive. The Groaner moaned in counterpoint to their cries.

He stopped by the freshwater pond first. Muskrat and kits had apparently survived the storm just fine. Eleven youngsters were out learning the art of catching snails and frogs. He watched for several minutes before the mother took alarm and whisked them off into hiding somewhere under the bank. As Loren passed Mussel Cove he caught sight of a tiny speck high above the swamp trees. He swung the glasses up to have a better look. Sure enough, it was an osprey — a fish hawk — fiercely intent on its hunting. As Loren watched, it sailed slowly down the shoreline towards him, resting on the wind. Suddenly, right above him, it came to a hovering stop in mid-air. Loren could see its tail flick open to a wide fan. In a flash, the hawk dove. It struck the water with feet outstretched, sending up a splash that totally concealed it from Loren's view for a fraction of a second. Then the powerful wings beat upward and it cleared the water, climbing rapidly, a shining fish impaled on its talons. It angled sharply inland and disappeared over the forest. It had a nest in the top of one of the highest firs. Loren had first seen it a couple of years ago when he had been up in the lighthouse searching the trees with his glasses. Each year the hawk had returned and rebuilt the same nest. Loren had tried to climb up to it several times, but had only gotten close enough to smell it. It stank of rotting fish. The nest itself looked like a scrap heap of twigs, dried seaweeds, pieces of broken wood, and driftwood of all shapes and sizes. There were nestlings in that nest, too, Loren was sure, but he hadn't been able to catch sight of them yet this year.

Four dots out on the ocean caught his attention and he turned the glasses on them. There were the fishing boats. Coming home really early today, he thought. Rolled and bunched in the sterns of three of them were the seines: the mackerel run was over for this season. Earlier than ever before.

When Loren returned home he found his father on the telephone. He hung up just as Loren came in. "That was Angus," he said. "He and Caleb are going out handlining for cod tomorrow. Wondered if you'd like to go with them. I said you probably would."

Loren knew his father too well to be deceived by his innocent look. William Randall had been disturbed by the rift between Caleb and Loren and he'd obviously decided it was time to do something about it.

Before Loren could think of a reason for refusing — he'd nearly always gone handlining with Caleb and Angus — his father went on. "We could use the fish. Guess you could use the money, too."

That was true. Any fish Loren caught handlining, he could sell himself. He was saving the money for university. Had quite a bit saved up already. He'd figured that handlining during summers while he was at high school, he'd have enough to cover his tuition by the time he was finished. But if he didn't go to high school…If he stayed here…He shook his head angrily. "Okay," he said, "I'll go."

The alarm went off at five o'clock the next morning. Loren had to force himself out of his narrow, but very soft, comfortable, and above all, warm bed. He staggered down the stairs and pulled the kettle over onto one of the electric burners. The woodfire was allowed to go out at night. Still only half-awake, he made tea. He was too sleepy to be hungry. He'd eat later in the boat. He opened the refrigerator, took out the lunch he had made the night before, then decided he was hungry after all. There was berry pie left over from supper, so he washed that down with a big glass of milk. A little more awake now, he pulled a heavy jacket on over his sweater. In the back entrance outside the kitchen he struggled into his oilpants and grabbed the lifejacket. He wouldn't put that on until he got into the boat, although it was bulky and awkward to carry. He knew that the minute he had it on and securely tied up, a certain spot on his back, right between his shoulder blades, would start to itch. No amount of telling himself it was all his imagination had ever been able to make it go away.

The other boats were already out by the time Loren got down to the wharf. Caleb was lugging a fish box down from the fish house; Loren went over to help him. As always, the cold, damp, sea-smelling early morning air, the cries of the gulls hunting in the mists, and the soft, lapping sounds of the water lifted his spirits. As they left the harbour, dawn was just beginning to break. Loren could barely make out the lighter shapes of the houses against the land. As always, the lighthouse stood silhouetted against the horizon, its beam flashing steadily, bright and strong now against the still-dark sky. The wind riffled through his hair, fresh against his face.

Loren set out the fish boxes — one for cod, one for haddock — while Angus steered. Caleb untied the painter and the stern lines in order to make the boat ready for fishing. Caleb and Loren baited the hooks, so the lines were ready to set out when they reached the fishing ground less than an hour later. Loren set the stern lines while Caleb and Angus set the head lines. Carefully, Loren lowered them into the water, one at a time. When he felt the lead touch bottom he hauled it up two fathoms, then tied the line to a ringbolt.

They were in luck today; the cod started biting almost immediately, and soon they were all busy hauling them in. Within a short time they had half-filled the cod box. Then the pickers took over: little pollock and sometimes haddock that could steal the bait without biting on the hook.

"We'll take a shift, boys. Get away from these pests." Angus started up the engine even as he spoke.

They pulled in the lines and, dragging anchor, set up again closer to Out Island.

Suddenly Caleb shouted. "I've got a big one! Loren, get the gaff!"

Slowly, heavily, Caleb hauled on the line. The fish, deep below, resisted sluggishly. Caleb started to pull it in, hand over hand, grimacing with the effort. Loren stood poised beside him, ready with the gaff, but no sooner did the fish come into view than it dove again with such speed and ferocity that Caleb was forced to give it line. The fish made a run for the bottom.

"It's a halibut!" Loren yelled. "Hang on to it, Caleb! Hang on to it!"

Caleb waited until the fish had finished its run and the tension eased somewhat on the line. Then he started hauling in again. Sweat stood out on his forehead and his eyes were almost squinted shut with the effort. He got the fish up to the boat once more, only to have it dive again.

"Let it go, Caleb. Give it line," Angus said quietly. "You'll have to tire him out before we'll get *that* one in."

The fish ran the line back to the bottom twice more before Caleb could finally get it up close enough.

"*Now*, Loren," he shouted. "The gaff! Get him!"

Loren tensed, judging the distance, then struck with the gaff and hooked it in the gills. The sudden strain on his arms almost made him lose his balance; then he and Caleb worked the fish into the boat together.

"Nice one," Angus said. "Fifty pounds if it's an ounce."

Loren and Caleb grinned at each other in triumph. At three dollars and fifty cents a pound, this would be a well-paid day's work.

They made a couple more shifts during the next hour or so, then brought out the lunches. The cod box was almost full, and they had their fair share of haddock as well.

Loren and Caleb sat side by side on the gunnel. Loren lifted his face to the sun. It was so warm he had taken off his sweater and lifejacket. He had the loop of a line around his hand, just feeling for a bite, but not really paying much attention. He had long ago perfected the technique of hauling a line and eating a sandwich at the same time. The Cape Islander rocked gently; in the distance the other three boats were just blobs of colour.

The CB suddenly sputtered.

"Frank? Got your ears on?" It was Uncle Lem.

There was no answer.

Uncle Lem called again. "Frank, you on channel?"

This time young Frank Parker answered. "Yeah, right here. I was just haulin' up a brown Tom cod."

"Well, then, you're doin' better than what I am," Uncle Lem replied. "I'm just havin' a mug-up, 'cause I can't get a stupid thing. Got about a dozen little haddock and half a box of cod that are only as big as skillies. Addin' up pretty slow."

"Know what you mean." Caleb's Uncle Forster broke in. "Little pollock are so thick over here they near lift the boat out of the water! Don't know how much longer I'll peg at it before I take a shift."

Loren and Caleb exchanged sly glances with Angus. Caleb's father made no move to get on the CB himself. Loyalty to friends and family didn't extend so far as to invite them over to share their good luck.

Suddenly Loren saw a fan-shaped spume of water shoot out of the sea about two hundred metres away. It was followed by another, then two more. First one, then four dark grey backs rolled out of the water, glistening wet in the sunlight.

"Fin whales!" Loren shouted.

The whales swam towards them, seemingly oblivious to the boat directly in their path. Loren knew they would turn, but he held his breath nonetheless as the huge animals powered their way lazily through the water. One surfaced less than a hundred metres away. Loren just had time to make out the small dorsal fin well to the rear of the body before the whale dove again. A cascade of water shot high up into the air. With one accord, all the whales turned and disappeared back out to sea. Loren breathed again.

"Man," said Caleb. "Wasn't that just something!"

"Seen them hundreds of times," Angus added. "Never do get over the sight of them, though."

After lunch, the dogfish took over. Sometimes they brought them up two at a time. They didn't keep them, of course. The dogfish was a shark and worthless to the fishermen. Finally, Angus had had enough.

"That's it for today, boys," he said. "Let's go home."

Caleb steered in while Angus began the job of cutting and gutting the cod. Loren helped him. When they had a box of guts, they'd throw them over, then sit back to watch the gulls drop screaming out of the sky to fight over them. Within seconds the water would be hidden by hundreds of flapping white wings, dozens more gulls hovering above and waiting their chance.

Back at Windward Island they ran the boat up onto the slipway, secured it for the night, gassed it up and washed it down, then took off their heavy jackets and set about dressing the cod in the old fish storehouse. They split them, salted them, cut out the tongues and cheeks. The haddock they would fillet last. Their halibut would go over to the mainland with the next boat.

As the boys worked, they kept glancing over at each

other. Caleb was two fish ahead. Loren found his hands working faster in order to catch up. Just when he thought he had, Caleb snuck a sideways look at him, grinned, and speeded up, too. Both boys were tearing into the fish as fast as their fingers could fly, and their old, friendly rivalry had taken over. As usual, Caleb just managed to stay ahead.

"And today won't be the day you can beat me, neither," he said triumphantly. Then he straightened up with an exaggerated sigh of exhaustion and staggered over to prime the pump. Sea water was pumped through a heavy hose for washing up. Loren washed down the table and floor and all the boxes they had used; then he turned the hose on himself and washed off his oilpants. He handed the hose to Caleb. The next moment a flood of icy-cold sea water streamed down into the back of his pants. He let out a strangled yell and whipped around.

Caleb dropped the hose and threw up his hands in mock self-defence. "It was an accident, Loren!" he cried. "Really!" But in spite of himself he burst out laughing. "If you could see the look on your face!" he shouted.

Loren grabbed for the hose and aimed it at the top of Caleb's oilpants. The next second Caleb was leaping over the floor, howling with the shock of the cold water. Loren began to laugh, too. Caleb made a grab for the hose, but only succeeded in soaking them both. They wrestled for it, sloshing in their boots and skidding over the slippery floor, until Angus put an end to the whole affair.

Still laughing, they slithered out of their oilpants, dumped the water, and hopped up behind the tractor to hitch a ride up to the Landrys' house.

Aunt Annie came out as soon as she heard their voices. "Your father's here, Loren. You're both invited to supper." Then she saw the state they were in. "What did you two do, then? Fall in the sea? Wait there until I bring you both some dry clothes, you foolish boys, you."

When he had changed, Loren followed Caleb into the kitchen. He could smell chicken roasting, and pots bubbled on the stove. A loaf of freshly baked bread sat on the counter, flanked by two steaming pies. Aunt Annie was rocking quietly in the rocker that her grandfather had made; Angus was sitting beside her in his favourite chair. They were watching "Three's Company" on the television that sat on the kitchen counter. The sound of TV laughter filled the warm, good-smelling room. Loren slid onto the couch that rested against the back wall of the kitchen, beside his father, and watched, too. He and his father, alone amongst the islanders, had no TV, and this was a treat.

After supper there were lines to rig and rusty hooks to sandpaper. Loren worked side by side with Caleb; neither said much, but it was a companionable silence.

It was almost like old times.

Chapter 7

THE WEATHER HELD and the fishing was good for the rest of the week. Loren was grateful that he and Caleb seemed to have reached a kind of truce, even if it was somewhat uneasy. On Monday of the following week, however, Angus was sick with a cold. This was unusual, but even more unusual was the fact that he couldn't help admitting it. Caleb exchanged a worried glance with Loren when, after lunch, Angus stopped fishing.

"I'll just rest in here for a while," Angus said, settling heavily onto the engine cover in the wheelhouse. "Just catch my breath for a bit." His breathing was laborious and he rubbed abstractedly at his chest.

"Do you have a pain?" Caleb asked quickly.

"No. No — not at all." Angus dropped his hand with a guilty air. "I'll be up in a minute." He coughed and, in spite of himself, his hand flew back to his chest.

For the rest of that day Caleb and Loren did all the work. They made a good team. They seemed to anticipate each other's needs without having to ask. The fish were biting well, but Caleb's worried look deepened when Loren suggested that they go in early and Angus didn't object. He was coughing continuously now.

"You take her in, Caleb," was all he said.

That night Caleb called to say that his father was feeling so poorly they wouldn't be taking the boat out the next day.

"It's not often Angus Landry misses a day's fishing because of ill health," Loren's father remarked with a frown.

Loren was worried, but it also gave him a respite. He enjoyed the fishing, and the money, but now he would have a day to do what he liked best — ramble around the island, see what was happening, beachcomb a bit. He needed a piece of driftwood for a perch. Uncle Angus was sure to be better in a day or two. After he'd caught up on the chores he packed a lunch, threw in a thermos of tea, and hoisted the light backpack onto his shoulders. Field glasses around his neck, notepad zippered into his jacket pocket, and he was off.

Although the sun was high and hot, the usual cool breeze was blowing in from the ocean. Loren sniffed the air like a happy hound dog and made for the swamp. He spent the rest of the morning sloshing around contentedly, then headed for the cranberry patch to eat his lunch. His mind was still taking notes as he skirted the Breakages and balanced across the sea wall beside the saltwater pond. He clambered up the hill, took the trail along the edge of the cliffs, and almost fell over April.

She was sitting just around a sharp bend in the path,

half-hidden by a juniper bush. As startled as Loren himself, she sprang to her feet. A large notebook fell into the bushes.

"What are you doing here?" Loren didn't mean the words to sound as harsh as they did, but they were out before he could collect himself.

"I suppose this is your private place, too, is it?"

Loren didn't have the nerve to say yes. "No..." he stuttered. "No...I just...I just..." To cover his confusion he leaned down and picked up the notebook.

It was a sketching pad. Outlined on it in pencil was the whole eastern tip of the island, cranberry bushes and all. The massive slate cliffs were drawn in boldly, rising from the froth and confusion of the waves. Along the cliff tops wind-blown spruces leaned away from the edge, branches straining for the security of the island forest. It was just a rough sketch, but the force of it was stunning.

Loren looked up, speechless. April made a grab for the pad.

"It's nothing!" she said quickly. "Give it back."

Loren hung on. "It's good. You never said you could draw!"

"I can't. I hate drawing. Really! I just fool around with it when I've nothing better to do." She snatched the book and hid it behind her back.

"It looked pretty good to me," Loren said. "Do you take lessons?"

"Oh, no. It was my mother who could draw. She was a *real* artist. You know, with shows and all? I couldn't ever do anything like that..." Her voice petered out.

"I don't know," Loren insisted. "If you can draw

73

that well without lessons or anything…seems to me you're pretty good. What does your dad say?"

"Dad!" The bitterness was back in her voice. "He'd laugh his head off if he ever thought I was trying to draw. He was so proud of my mother — he'd think I was being ridiculous."

"But still…" Loren couldn't leave it alone.

April glared at him. "Drop it. I really don't want to talk about it, okay?"

Loren shrugged. He was learning that when April didn't want to talk about something, you didn't push. "Okay, have it your way." He walked over to the cliff edge. "How did you find this place, anyway?" he asked.

April's face cleared and she relaxed. "Oh, I've been exploring whenever I can get away from that horrible house. It's amazing. I never paid much attention to the outdoors, but you wouldn't believe how many cool things there are on this island!"

Loren broke into a grin. "I've lived here all my life, remember?"

April blushed. It was easier to tell this time — she didn't have so much make-up on. She made a face. "Yeah — right. Dumb me. As usual."

"Not so dumb," Loren disagreed. "Have you had lunch?"

"No. I'd better get back."

"Wait. I've got two sandwiches and some tea. Share with me." Before she could refuse, Loren started to rummage through his knapsack. "Come on. Here." He held out a slightly squashed sandwich. "It's fish. There wasn't anything else handy when I left this morning."

"A cold fish sandwich? You've got to be kidding!"

"It's good. Lots of mayonnaise and lemon. Try it."

April sat down beside him and looked at the sandwich dubiously. "I don't *believe* I'm going to eat this." She closed her eyes and took a bite.

Loren watched, still grinning, as she chewed.

Finally she opened her eyes again. "It's not the best thing I've ever eaten," she said. "But I guess I've had worse." She took another bite.

They finished their sandwiches and the thermos of tea. Loren heaved a huge sigh of satisfaction and stretched himself out in the sunlight, nose down. Seen this close, the cranberry bush mats were alive with tiny black ants, climbing and reclimbing their individual green-bladed mountains. Loren poked out a finger and encouraged one to climb over it; then he rested his head on his arms. April sat beside him, staring out to sea. Loren wondered idly what she was thinking about. Then, with the sound of the surf pounding rhythmically away, and the sun beating down so strongly it seemed to warm every bone in his body, he closed his eyes and almost fell asleep.

After a while April stretched and picked up her sketch pad. "I guess I should be getting back," she said regretfully. "There's still a pile of work to do in that house."

"I'll walk with you," Loren said, getting to his feet and dusting off his pants and jacket. "Show you a short cut through the forest."

A narrow path led from the cliff edge into the trees. Unless you knew where to look for it, it would be hard to find; the trees and bushes presented an almost impenetrable barrier. Loren pushed through, then held back some branches so that April could follow him. One moment they had been standing in hard, bright sunlight with their ears full of the crashing of the waves, and the next instant, as the bushes closed behind them, they found themselves in a dim, velvet hush of shadows, with only the whisper of a now-muted sea in their ears. The narrow path led through moss- and lichen-covered trees. Ferns uncurled softly on either side. They came to a fallen, rotting fir. Loren reached back to help April, but she had already climbed over it herself, nimble in spite of Amy's boots. The path became marshy and wet as they skirted the swamp.

Suddenly April tripped and fell sprawling. She grimaced as she saw mud on her once-white pants. "What kind of animal made that, anyway?" She pointed to the small round hole in the path that had tripped her up.

"That's a Carey hole," Loren answered.

"A what?"

"A Carey hole — a hole made by a bird," Loren said.

April looked at him incredulously. "You really want me to believe a *bird* dug this hole?"

Loren laughed. "Yep. Mother Carey's chickens, we call them, but they're really storm petrels. Usually they stay out over the ocean, but they come in to breed on the land. They make a tunnel in the ground, like this one, and the female lays one egg in it. Then the male and the female take turns sitting on it while the other one goes fishing. Job-sharing, sort of."

"There's a *bird* down in there." April looked at

Loren to see if he was trying to make a fool of her.

"Honest, there is. Look — kneel down and smell it."

"Smell it!"

"Yes. Go on."

"Now I know you're putting me on," April said, but she crouched down and put her nose to the hole. "Yuck!" She jumped back up quickly.

"Stink birds, we call them. You don't want to reach in and try to get one out," Loren said. "My brother Walt did once and his hand smelled so bad he could hardly get the stench off, even by washing. Must be a kind of protection for them, I guess. Keeps animals from being tempted to dig down there."

April shook her head. "Birds in holes. Who would believe it?"

They came out of the forest just by the beach and turned onto the narrow dirt road that led back to the lighthouse. As they scuffed along in the dust, a sudden flurry caught April by surprise and she nearly tripped again. The road seemed to erupt into small fluffy balls of dust and a shrill cry grated in their ears.

"Now what?" April exclaimed.

"Sandpiper babies," Loren answered. "That's their mother telling them to run and hide. Look." He pointed.

April burst into laughter. The birdlings had run and buried their heads in the nearest bush. Four tiny, feathered rumps stuck out.

When they reached Loren's house April started to say goodbye, but Loren stopped her. "April," he said hesitantly, "if you're not in too much of a hurry…"

She looked at him curiously. Now it was his turn

to blush. For a moment he paused, about to change his mind, then went on. "I mean," he said, "you might like to come and see something. I can't draw or anything, but I carve."

"Carve?"

"Birds." Loren's embarrassment deepened, but he forced himself to go on. "Would you like to see them?"

"Sure. Great!"

They went in through the back door, shedding boots and jackets in the kitchen entranceway. Loren led the way up to his room, opened the door and stood back. His heart was pounding and the palms of his hands felt sweaty. What was he doing, anyway?

April went on past him, then drew in her breath with a gasp. "Loren!" She turned back to him, her eyes shining. "You made all these?"

Loren nodded. "Here, let me show you." Sheepishly, he picked up a just-begun carving of a cedar waxwing. It had a berry in its beak. He'd seen a row of cedar waxwings on a tree branch the week before, carefully passing just such a berry down the line and then back up again.

Then the baby heron caught April's eye. "This is *so* great! Do they *really* look like this? I mean — all gawky and lumpy like this? I *love* it. What is it?"

She stayed for almost an hour. Loren showed her everything he had made and told her about each one. All the while she held the carving of the baby heron in her hand, stroking it and patting it absent-mindedly. As she turned to go, she reluctantly put it back on the desk.

"Take it," Loren said.

"What?"

"Really. Take it."

April shook her head. "Loren, I can't. It must have taken you ages to make. I can't take it."

Loren felt stupid and tongue-tied. He'd only ever given one carving away before, and that had been to Walt. Nevertheless, he stubbornly repeated, "Please, April, I'd like you to have it."

As carefully as if it had been a real bird that would take flight if startled, April reached for the heron. She cradled it in her palms. "Thank you." Her voice was so quiet he could hardly hear her. "Thank you, Loren."

The next day Loren was up to his ears in chores. He weeded the garden all morning and into the afternoon until the fog started wisping in. When the foghorn started its plaint, and the fog became so thick he couldn't even see the back porch of the house, he gave up.

Footsteps on the back porch, then a knock at the kitchen door, interrupted him just as he was putting the kettle on for tea. Before he could open the door, Caleb burst in.

"April's lost!" he gasped.

Chapter 8

"April's lost?" Even as he spoke, Loren was grabbing for his slicker and shoving his feet into his boots. He saw her perched on the cliff edge, sketching. If the fog had caught her out there…The paths along the cliffs could be treacherous if you didn't know them well. Cracks and fissures cut through them unexpectedly; the crumbling slate offered dangerously unsure footing.

"Her dad's on the mainland for a couple of days and she's staying with us," Caleb answered. "She went out this morning and said she'd be back at noon for dinner, but she hasn't turned up. Fog's so thick she'll never find her way. We've searched our end of the island," he went on, following Loren out the door, "but she's nowhere there."

"I've got an idea where she might be," Loren answered. "We were up at the eastern end yesterday — maybe she went back there."

Caleb stopped short. "She was with you yesterday?" he frowned. "We were some worried when she didn't show up for lunch. That's why she promised for sure she'd be back on time today. Why was she with *you*?"

Caleb's tone annoyed Loren. He pulled Caleb forward. "Why don't you just shut up, Caleb? Let's get going. Why shouldn't she be with me? You think you own her? Come *on*," he snapped as Caleb still hung back. "I'll take the cliff path, you cut through the forest."

The fog was not friendly today. It lay thick and heavy all over the island. The foghorn sounded muted and far away; even the normal roar and rush of the waves was deadened. Loren hurried along the cliff path as quickly as he dared. Like most other things on the island, the path changed every day with the wind and the weather: small landslides, erosions, bushes growing, trees falling.

Loren followed the shore down along Mussel Cove, then started the climb back up towards the Breakages on the southeastern tip of the island. He could take the narrow trail along the cliff edge, instead of skirting inland through the swamp, as he usually did. If April were farther along, where the cranberry bushes were, this would be the quickest way to get there. The path barely clung to the cliff edge in places, but Loren had been over it before searching for birds' nests. He was sure-footed and had no fear of heights.

He forced his way along the path, sometimes holding onto the splintery branches of broken, dead trees to keep his balance. The fog was so thick he could only see an arm's length in front of him. Down to the right he could hear the breakers. The path grew even more narrow. Suddenly, it wasn't there at all. It was just where the eastern tip dipped down to the saltwater pond. If there had been no fog, Loren would have been able to see the pond and the sea wall, and the land rising again on the other side up to the forest and the cranberry bushes; but now all he could see were the reaching, skeletal arms of the trees, stretching out from the jumble that was the Breakages. White blending into white fog. As he hesitated, he heard a noise. Something was crashing around in there. Right in the middle, by the sound of it. He held himself absolutely still and listened intently. Silence. Then, there it was again. No animal who lived in there would be so clumsy.

"April! Is that you?" His voice seemed to be caught by the fog and die. "April!" he called again, louder.

"Loren!" The cry was so faint he thought he had imagined it. Then it came again, stronger, with a note of panic in it. "Loren! Where are you? I can't see anything!"

"I'm coming," Loren called back. "Don't panic. I'm coming for you. Keep calling so I can find you."

"Here! I'm over here!"

Loren searched desperately for a way into the tangle of dead branches and trunks — the one spot on the island that wasn't honeycombed with paths, since no one ever ventured in here. Finally he found a patch that wasn't as tangled as the rest. If he stooped down...He pushed through it, then found his way barred by an enormous fallen trunk. He stepped up on a branch to get over it and the dead wood broke with a crack that reverberated even through the fog. The next instant he was lying on his back beside the tree. There was a pain in his left leg and a long rip in his pants, with blood slowly seeping into it.

Just then April called again. Loren pushed himself to a sitting position and shouted back. She sounded nearer. Heartened, he struggled to his feet and tackled the log once more. This time he made it over and saw to his relief that the trees thinned out a bit in front of him.

"April," he called. "Shout out again."

She did, somewhere just straight ahead of him. His leg was stinging and the blood was soaking into his pants, but he pushed through the underbrush frantically. By the sound of April's voice she was near hysteria.

"I'm coming, April," he yelled. "Keep on calling me. I'll be with you soon."

She was sobbing now more than calling. If he hadn't been so close he wouldn't have been able to hear her at all. Branches and sharp-edged twigs tore at his hands and his face.

Finally, he pushed through into a small clearing. Huddled against the trunk of a fallen tree, just visible in the shroudlike fog, was April. Her face was buried in her hands. Loren ran towards her, almost tripping over an exposed root, then sank down beside her and put his arms around her. Now she broke down completely and clung to him, face buried in his jacket.

"Oh, Loren! I was so scared! I was so *scared*!"

"Sh. Hush. It's all right. It's all right now." Loren soothed her like an injured bird. "April, stop crying. It's all right now."

Gradually the sobs subsided, but April was shaking violently. Her light jacket was soaked through. Loren took off his slicker and wrapped it around her. He patted and hushed and calmed her. Finally, she could talk.

"How in the world did you get in here?" Loren asked then. "Where were you trying to go?"

"I went up to that spot where we were yesterday to..." She stopped. "Well, anyway," she went on, "I went up there, and it was so sunny and warm and peaceful..." She stopped again with a hiccup. "I lay down and I guess I went to sleep. When I woke up the fog was coming in. I don't know...I just saw it coming in at me, over the sea like that...I guess I panicked." She caught her breath and shuddered. "Anyway, I'd come along the cliff path from the beach on the other side like I did before, but with the fog I didn't dare go back that way, so I thought I'd try to find that path we took yesterday. You know, through the forest?" She looked up at Loren. Her face was muddy, scratched, and tear-stained. Any make-up she might have had on was long since gone.

Loren reached into his pocket, took out a tissue, and dabbed at a spot of blood on her cheek, his own leg forgotten.

"Suddenly there was sort of water all around," April went on with another hiccup. "It was all squishy and I nearly lost a boot. I tried to keep on going, but it just got worse and worse."

"Swamp," Loren said. "You got yourself into Low Swamp. You have to know what you're doing in there."

"Well, I sure didn't. I tried to find my way back to where I had started, but the fog was so thick. That fog, Loren…" Her voice began to rise. She caught herself.

Loren waited for a moment, and she went on.

"I couldn't hear the sea, I couldn't see anything but fog…I just kept pushing on and on and suddenly I was here. What is this place? Why are the trees all dead?"

"We call it the Breakages. I don't really know why so many trees have died along this stretch. Maybe it's because the southeasterlies bring so much salt-water spray up onto them. We never come here, though."

April shivered. "I can see why. I couldn't get out, Loren. I just kept going around and around, and I couldn't get out!"

"Well, we'll get out now," Loren said. "Do you feel up to walking?"

"Anything," April answered fervently. "Anything to get out of this place."

Then it occurred to Loren that he'd been crashing around in there after April for so long, he'd totally lost track of directions as well. There was nothing in here to guide him, and the fog was getting thicker by the minute. Something in his face must have betrayed his sudden doubts to April.

"Loren! We can get out, can't we?" She was starting to get panicky again. "You *do* know the way out?"

"Of course I do." Loren's voice was just a shade too loud. "Of course I do," he repeated, trying to sound normal. At worst we'll just stumble around in here for a while, he reassured himself, but he shivered. Without his slicker the fog seemed to be seep-

ing into his very bones. It was hard to remember
that it was summer. He was aware of the gash in his
leg now, too, and it was hurting.

Loren got to his feet, stood still and took stock of
the situation. Very, very faintly, he imagined he could
hear the sea. It seemed to be at his back. That would
mean that the swamp was in front of them. Probably
April hadn't come in very far. Loren knew every inch
of that swamp and could easily guide them through
it and back towards the lighthouse and the other
houses.

"This way." With an effort he made his voice sound
confident and matter-of-fact.

He went ahead of April, trying to make a path for
her, but dead, brittle branches can't be held back the
way live, bending ones can. After only a few metres
they were both covered in newly bleeding scratches.
Nevertheless, April kept up. Her breath was coming
in frightened gasps, but she stuck grimly behind
Loren. Just when he was beginning to be terribly
afraid he had guessed wrongly, the ground began to
slope downwards and become marshy. Suddenly, as
if breaking through a barrier, they were out of the
Breakages and into the wet, living swamp.

"It's okay now." Loren allowed himself an audible
sigh of relief. "With Amy's boots on you won't even
get wet feet. Just follow me and walk where I do."

Halfway through the swamp he paused. "See this
big old tree here?" he asked.

April looked up.

"Up in the top. See the nest? You can just make it
out. Sort of a blur up there. That's your baby heron's
nest."

"Really?" April looked back at him and broke into a smile.

"Yeah," Loren answered. "Nobody home now, though." He reached back for her hand to help her around a stump and they went on.

By the time they stumbled into Loren's house they were both shaking with cold. Loren's father was sitting in the kitchen.

"You found her! Thank goodness! Annie called and told me you were out looking for her. You should have let me know. You just disappeared all of a sudden."

"I never even thought…," Loren began, dismayed. "When Caleb came here and said April was lost, I never even thought…I just lit out to find her."

"Well, anyway, thank heaven you did find her. Come on in here by the stove, both of you, and get warm. You look half-frozen. Loren, what have you done to your leg?"

Loren looked down. The blood had dried into a solid mass. "I fell. It's not so bad."

His father moved the kettle onto the hot burner, then pulled out a chair for April. "Sit here, April. Loren, you'd better go get those pants off and we'll have a look at that leg. I'll call Annie and let her know April's safe. Where's Caleb?"

Where indeed? Loren's stomach turned over and his ribs felt like they were caving in as he realized he'd been so intent on getting April back home, he'd forgotten completely about Caleb.

"He was going to look in the forest," he began

weakly. Why hadn't he remembered to give him a shout when they'd reached the swamp? Caleb would surely have heard him. He hadn't thought about Caleb once. He'd have to go back and find him.

He started for the door, ignoring his father's quick protest, but before he could reach it, Caleb's exhausted, wet face appeared. "Uncle William," he began, "I can't..." He stopped. "Loren! April!" He gaped at them. "What are you doing here?"

Loren took a step backwards. "I...I found her," he began hesitantly. "In the Breakages."

"Why didn't you call for me? Why didn't you find me and tell me? You knew where I was. You knew where I'd be looking."

"I was in such a hurry to get April back...I guess...I guess I just forgot."

"You FORGOT!" Caleb roared. "I've been trailing around getting freezing cold and soaking wet, and you've been sitting here all warm and comfortable, and you FORGOT?"

"Look, I'm sorry. Really I am."

Caleb grabbed Loren by the shirt as if to hit him. "You're a fine friend, you," he shouted, and shook Loren as hard as he could.

Loren heard the fabric tear. At that, something seemed to tear inside, as well.

"Who are you to be talking about fine friends?" he shouted back. "You're the one who took a perfect stranger up to our treehouse! You're the one who told my father what I was planning to do when it was none of your business! And you're the one who's more worried about a perfect stranger who's stupid enough to get herself lost in the fog than about the

fact that this is probably our last summer here together!"

"Thanks a lot, Loren." The clear, angry voice
startled them. "I'm sorry I've been so much trouble.
This 'perfect stranger' is going home. Are you coming, Caleb?"

Chapter 9

Loren had barely finished doing the breakfast dishes the next morning when the telephone rang.

"Loren? It's Annie. Loren, Uncle Angus is really sick. The doctor on the mainland says to bring him over right away, but all the men have gone out hand-lining. Will you come help Caleb with the boat?" Aunt Annie's voice was tight; she didn't sound like her usual breezy self.

"I'll be right over." Loren hung up and hurried down the hall to his father's study. "Dad," he called out, "Uncle Angus is sick. He has to go to the doctor, and Aunt Annie wants me to go over to the mainland with them to help Caleb with the boat."

William Randall looked up from his desk. "He must be pretty bad. I can't remember the last time Angus ever even admitted to feeling poorly, let alone allowed himself to be taken to the mainland to a doctor."

"Aunt Annie sounds worried." Loren was feeling stunned. Uncle Angus was a rock. It was unthinkable that anything should happen to him.

By the time he reached the wharf they were there

and waiting for him. Angus was sitting in the boat, slumped on the engine cover in the wheelhouse. His face was flushed and puffy and he was breathing in short, obviously painful gasps. When he saw Loren, he snorted. "Foolishness, Mother, that's what it is. Foolishness. You didn't need to bother Loren." The words ended in a wheeze and a deep, racking cough. Beads of perspiration stood out on his forehead.

Aunt Annie patted his shoulder. "Hush, Angus," she said quietly. "Loren doesn't mind."

"Of course not."

Loren and Caleb stared at each other coldly. April wouldn't even look at him. She unhooked the boat and the three of them pushed it down the slipway, which was kept well greased with cod oil. April hopped in while Loren held the lines. In a moment Caleb had the engine started up and Loren jumped in, balancing himself against the open door of the wheelhouse, as Caleb slowly reversed and turned the boat.

The mainland was a smudge on the horizon. Caleb glanced up at the radar beside the wheel and adjusted their course minutely. The CB crackled. Call letters came through loudly, then the voice of Uncle Forster.

"Are you on your way, then, Caleb?" he asked. "Do you need any help?"

"No, thank you, Uncle Forster," Caleb replied. "We're fine."

"How's Angus?"

"Not too well," Caleb said with an anxious look down at his father.

"Well, I'm headin' for in now. Weather's comin'

up a bit dirty. Watch for it on your way back, you."

"I will, Uncle Forster."

"I'll be monitoring the CB. Call if you need me."

"I will," Caleb repeated. "Thanks."

"Good enough."

Caleb replaced the microphone and turned his attention back to the boat. The outlines of West Harbour were just beginning to show through a light, leftover haze.

As soon as they had the boat docked and made fast, Aunt Annie got their old station wagon out of the garage beside the wharf. They helped Angus onto the seat beside her.

"I'll drop you three at the shopping centre, then take Angus on to the doctor's," Annie said. "Caleb, you know what we need. We'll meet you at McDonald's as soon as we're through."

"Good enough," Caleb answered. He looked at his father uncertainly.

"We'll be fine," Annie said gently. "Get on with you."

"I hope...you know...I hope you'll be okay," April said to Angus.

" 'Course I will," Angus answered gruffly. "Doctor'll probably laugh his head off at me coming all this way in for nothing. *And* then prescribe a fortune's worth of pills!" He started to cough again.

Aunt Annie shifted the car into gear impatiently. "Make sure you get everything, Caleb," she said. "I want to be getting back as soon as possible." She drove off so quickly the tires squealed.

"My mom, the hot-rodder," Caleb joked weakly. Then he turned to April. "I have to go to the supermarket and then the drugstore. Want to come?"

"Sure," April answered. "There's a pile of stuff I need." They both turned to look at Loren. There was an instant of silence.

"I've got things to do," he said stiffly. "I'll meet you at McDonald's."

Caleb nodded curtly. He grabbed April's arm and they darted across the parking lot towards the stores.

Loren looked after them, then started across, too, more slowly. He hadn't had time to ask his father if there was anything they needed, and he couldn't think of a thing. By the time he reached the mall doors, April and Caleb had disappeared. He pushed open the heavy door and went in. A blast of cool, stale air hit him. As he stood irresolutely in the entrance, a large, bustling man bumped into him.

"Excuse me..." Loren began, but the man was already halfway down the corridor. Loren turned and stepped right in front of a woman racing along pushing a baby stroller, which caught him squarely on the place where he'd hurt his leg. He let out a grunt of pain.

"Why don't you watch where you're going?" the woman said crossly, angling the stroller swiftly up on its two back wheels and changing direction sharply.

"Excuse me..." Loren began again, but she had already whizzed by, the sleeping baby undisturbed by the sudden encounter.

Loren headed for a bench and looked around him. Everything he hated most: Idiot music — as Walt used to call the bland stuff they pipe into stores and elevators — was coming out of a speaker right above his head. From a record store a blast of rock music competed with it. The ashtray beside him was stuffed with cigarettes, one butt still smoking and giving off a foul stench. Half-empty, soggy coffee cups sitting in muddy puddles and crumpled soft-drink cans filled the wastebasket to overflowing. Children tagged at their mothers' heels or ran ahead shrieking. Kids hung around the snack stands or paraded past in packs. Couples lounged by, talking earnestly. One small child — a girl? a boy? — in denim shorts and T-shirt and cropped-off, ragged blond hair, suddenly came to a full stop in front of Loren. For a moment they stared at each other; then a hand with chipped purple nail polish whisked the child out of Loren's field of vision. Loren closed his eyes. He had at least an hour. What to do? Library or bookstore. They seemed to be the only alternatives. Both were at the very opposite end of the mall.

The bookstore was wall-to-wall people. There were racks of paperbacks, racks of mass-market children's books, tables of best-sellers, shelves of how-to books. Loren stopped short. *How to Build a Bunny*? Surely not. He leaned over and took a closer look. Sure enough. The large, glossy book gave instructions on how to build wooden animal playhouses in your back yard, bunny included. It was full of beautiful photographs and cost seventy-five dollars. The whole treehouse hadn't cost that much.

The tiny library wasn't much better. Right in the middle was a woman reading a story to a group of young children. Loren browsed along the shelves a bit, stepping over, around, and once, by accident, on children, then selected a book. He found a chair back in the corner and settled down to read.

After a while he gave up and listened to the story-teller. The older children started staring at him, and when the blond child that he had seen earlier sat down on the floor beside him, Loren decided to leave.

He made his way slowly back to McDonald's. As he was about to push his way through the door, he caught sight of Caleb and April sitting at a table. Caleb was talking earnestly, and April was nodding in apparent agreement. Suddenly, for a moment, Caleb looked like a complete stranger. Loren stared as if he had never seen him before. Then he turned on his heel and left.

He was sitting on a bench outside, waiting, when he saw the Landrys' car pull up. Aunt Annie was alone.

"He's had to go into hospital, Loren." There was a stricken look on her face. "Pneumonia. The doctors say it's bad."

By the time they got back to the boat it was raining heavily and the wind was gusting.

"I don't know...maybe we should stay over tonight. We could stay with Gran..." Aunt Annie's parents had a small house in West Harbour. She looked at the whitecaps dubiously.

"We've crossed in a lot worse weather than this, Mom," Caleb answered.

"You're right, of course, Caleb. But without your father..." She hesitated. "There's so many things I have to get from home, though, and take to Dad tomorrow. Do you think you and Loren can manage?"

"We can manage." Caleb didn't bother to consult

Loren. "We'll just hurry now before it gets any worse." He took his mother's hand and gave her a hug as he helped her into the boat. "He'll be all right, Mom, you'll see. Nothing can get him down for long."

"And with all the modern medicines and stuff...They'll have him better in no time, Aunt Annie," April added. She jumped into the boat and put her arm around the older woman while Caleb and Loren made ready to cast off. Aunt Annie stood with her back to the island, staring through the rain towards the mainland long after it had disappeared into the distance.

"Loren, see if you can get Uncle Forster on the CB, will you?" Caleb asked. His voice was cold and polite. "He should know we're on our way back." He stood at the wheel, the window open in spite of the lashing rain. His eyes alternated between the heaving seas in front of him and the radar hanging from the roof of the cabin up to his left. The boat hurled itself into the waves with a furious, confident abandon. Up it rode, onto a crest; then, with a curious, sideslipping motion of its flat keel, it plunged into a trough. Then up it went again, to start all over. Loren repeated their call numbers into the CB microphone over and over, but only a staticky crackle answered him. Finally he gave up, but left the channel open. Automatically, he moved with the motion of the boat, his eyes following Caleb's out to sea and then to the radar. Ahead was a moving white curtain of wind and rain — impossible to see through — but on the radar screen the unmistakable shape of their island grew steadily closer. The foghorn blew regularly, reassuringly.

They had been out with Angus in much worse weather than this, and Loren knew Caleb was capable of handling it. In fact, in other circumstances he would even have been enjoying the trip. Then he caught sight of April's face. She was holding tightly to Aunt Annie, on the other side of the wheelhouse. At that moment Caleb turned his head and saw her also.

"Great, eh?" he shouted with a huge grin. Water from the open window ran down his face in streams.

April managed a faint, sickly smile. "You mean we're not drowning?"

Caleb roared with laughter. "Long way from that, you! Come on over here and I'll show you how the radar works."

April looked dubious, then very reluctantly let go of Aunt Annie. Hanging onto the cabin wall and anything else that offered a handhold, she made her way around the engine cover to stand beside Caleb. Loren moved out of her way, but she didn't seem to notice him. She stared out the window at the mountainous waves rising in front of them, wind-whipped and wild, then let out a small shriek and grabbed for support as they fell into yet another trough.

Caleb laughed again. He put his arm around her shoulders to steady her. "See the island?" he yelled into her ear, and nodded towards the radar. "There's our harbour, dead ahead."

April looked up at the radar, then back at Caleb. Just then the CB barked into life.

"Caleb, are you there?" It was Uncle Forster. At Caleb's nod, Loren took down the mike.

"Here, Uncle Forster. It's Loren."

"Are you all right, then? Whereabouts are you?"

"Coming up to the harbour now, Uncle Forster. We're fine."

"Good enough. I'll just come down to help you with the boat when you're in, then."

"Thanks, Uncle Forster. See you in a few minutes."

Loren replaced the microphone, then turned to April, ready to offer some encouragement. She was clinging to Caleb like a leech. She gasped involuntarily as they met another towering wave, but the tight, terrified look was gone from her face. As the boat dropped, she braced her feet wide and allowed herself to go with the motion. Another wave loomed. April took a deep breath and steadied herself, loosening her hold on Caleb. They crested it. Then, as they plunged sideways and downwards again, she let out the breath with a sound that was almost a whoop. In the brief interval before the next wave, she looked up at Caleb and grinned.

"You could almost get used to this!"

"You sure could," he answered with an equally big grin. "There's no better ride at the Exhibition!"

As soon as they had run the boat up onto the slipway, taken out the plug to drain it, and secured it for the night, April caught Caleb's arm and started up the path with him. "You know..." Now she was almost bubbling over. "I've always been sort of scared of boats. Didn't really like them at all. But out there...It was *grand!* I can't believe it. It really was!" She was still chattering as they walked on, leaving

Aunt Annie and Loren to follow behind.

"Thanks for coming with us, Loren," Aunt Annie said. "Forster will take me in tomorrow, won't you, Forster?"

The older man nodded. "Sure enough," he said.

"It was no problem, Aunt Annie. Anything I can do, just let me know," Loren answered quickly. "Give Uncle Angus my love. Tell him I hope he gets better soon…" His words trailed off. Caleb and April were turning into Caleb's house. Neither had bothered to say goodbye.

Chapter 10

LOREN WAS HALFWAY down the stairs the next morning when he heard voices coming from the kitchen. Mr. McIvor. What was the man after now? The urge to find out was strong, but stronger still was the desire to avoid him. Loren could feel his stomach knotting up. He went out the front door, headed up towards the field by the lighthouse, and threw himself on the ground.

The wind from the north brought the warm, slightly foreign smell of the mainland drifting across the island. Soon the back door of the house opened and Mr. McIvor came out. Loren watched him walk jauntily down the path towards the wharf.

He hadn't had breakfast, but made no move to go back to the house. He wasn't hungry any more. He lay for so long, unmoving, that two pheasant chicks emerged from the long grass and began making their way towards him with short, quick bursts of movement. Suddenly there was a shrill call from the mother, hidden somewhere out of Loren's sight. The two chicks froze and instantly became invisible. The next moment, Caleb appeared, cutting across the field.

"Uncle William said you might be up here."

Loren waited.

"I wanted to talk to you."

"Why?"

"I talked to Dad on the telephone this morning."

"How is he?"

"Says he's feeling better already. Not too happy, though. They've got him all trussed up in some bed, and nurses fussing around him to beat the band. He hates it. But the doctors say he'll be okay."

"I'm glad."

Loren's mind was racing. Could Caleb have come up to apologize? If so, he'd meet him halfway — more than halfway. This bad feeling between them was frightening. If Caleb went off to school with both of them feeling like this...

"He's going to be there for a fair while, though, they say," Caleb went on. "That's what I wanted to talk to you about. Since the handlining's been so good and all, he told me that you and I could take the boat out by ourselves while he's in the hospital, if we want."

Loren looked at Caleb incredulously. Angus had never let any of his sons take the boat out alone until they were at least seventeen. "By ourselves?"

"Yeah. Look..." Caleb seemed to be searching for words. "Well, I do want to keep on fishing, and I do need the money, and...and I can't go out by myself..."

"So that's it," Loren said acidly. "And here I thought you'd come up to apologize."

"Apologize? Me? What have *I* got to apologize for?

You're the one didn't even bother to let me know you'd found April!"

"And *you're* the one that's been messing things up for me all summer!" Loren exploded.

They glared at each other. Then Caleb spoke again, even more angrily. "Okay, don't come then. It seems pretty stupid, though, letting the boat sit there idle when we could be out making money with it."

Loren hesitated. Caleb was right. Uncle Angus might not be well enough to go out again for weeks, and they'd just be wasting time. Still...

The silence lengthened. Finally, Loren shrugged. "Oh, all right. I'll go." It wouldn't be much fun, sitting out in the boat every day with things bad and getting worse between them, but at least he'd be fishing.

"Good enough," Caleb said shortly and headed down the hill.

The weather held clear, the fishing was good, and Loren and Caleb went out nearly every day. Both boys spoke as little as possible and went about it all as if they were just doing a job. Even when a seal's head popped up in the wake of their boat, Loren didn't say a word to Caleb. Caleb obviously saw it cavorting after them, too, but didn't mention it either.

Late one afternoon, when they were trudging silently up the path from the wharf, loaded down with pails of fish, Auntie Pearl waylaid them. She flew out her kitchen door as they passed by and waved a kitchen towel at them.

"Caleb! Loren! Hot apple pie!"

No matter what their problems, no one bypassed Auntie Pearl's pies. They shucked their slickers and boots at the kitchen door and left the pails of fish on the porch. Uncle Lem was holding forth to someone.

"Oh, no, fishin' wit' my father here on the island wasn't good enough for me, you. I wanted to go out on a big vessel. I can still see them big white sails billowin', the flags all flyin' — that was somethin' pretty to see. So off I run one day and shipped out as a flunky. Eleven years old, I was. Youngest boy on the ship."

April was perched on a chair beside the sturdy wooden table. She looked up and waved as they came in, then turned her attention back to Uncle Lem. She looked slightly confused, but a cleanly scraped plate in front of her testified to the fact that she'd been first at the pie.

"Now just pull up some chairs there." Auntie Pearl bustled the boys in and cut them each a steaming quarter-pie slice. She put the rest of the pie down on the table. "You'll be wanting some cream," she announced as she slathered half a pitcherful of heavy cream onto their plates.

"Flunky, catchy, same thing. Always the youngest boy. Had to cut out the tongues and the cheeks. My father was some mad when he found out, but it was too late. I was off. Gone for two, three months."

Auntie Pearl broke in. "You been out in the boat fishin' yet, my girl?"

"No...not fishing. I went to the mainland in it, though."

"I knowed nothin', I'm tellin' you," Uncle Lem

went on. "You had to learn pretty quick, though. And it'd only be the odd feller'd be good to you — take the time to show you things. You didn't learn fast — you messed up too much — you got hit. Plain and simple. By God, I learned some fast, I'll tell you."

"My days, women never went out in the boats," Auntie Pearl continued. "But nowadays, things is sure changed. Lady reporter came down this way last summer — spent all day every day out on the boats with the men for a whole week."

"The weather was some dirty that year, you. Storms one after the other. T'underin' and lightnin' heavy more times than not. By God, you worked for what you got. And that weren't much, you."

"Don't know how she managed about the bathroom, but I guess she must have figured somethin' out."

April was looking from one to the other like a spectator at a tennis match. Caleb and Loren just tucked into their pie and let the conversation roll over them. They were used to Uncle Lem and Auntie Pearl carrying on simultaneous conversations about different subjects.

"Well, would you look at that!" Uncle Lem suddenly exclaimed, staring out the window and pulling the lace curtain back a bit to have a better view. "There's young Frank. Runnin' up the path. Wonder what bit him?"

"Why don't you show the boys that pretty picture you made?" Auntie Pearl asked.

April looked across at Loren in dismay. "Oh, no! I mean...they wouldn't want to see that!"

"Well, I guess they would." Auntie Pearl turned to

the boys. "Found her sittin' out back by the field, drawin' a picture of our old house, if you please. Now I never did see nothin' particular about this place, although it's been a good home for a good many years, but she made it as pretty as could be."

"You draw?" Caleb looked up from his pie.

"No," April protested. "Not really..."

"Show it," Auntie Pearl insisted.

Uncle Lem let the curtain drop and settled back down into his chair. "Must have gone foolish, that boy," he said, shaking his head. "Just because it's comin' on to rain a little. What's he want to go runnin' around like that for?" He turned his attention back to Caleb and Loren. "Just make a long arm for that pie, there, you boys."

"No, thanks, Uncle Lem," Caleb answered, pushing away his empty plate and sighing deeply. "I'm full to the scupper holes."

Loren considered another piece, then decided he couldn't manage it, either.

Uncle Lem looked at April. "How about you, then?"

"No, thanks. I couldn't. Really."

"Well, then." He went on with his story. "We had a bad time of it that year, let me tell you. Storm after storm. Lost two men in one o' them. How that vessel rolled! Come time to head for in, finally, we was heavin', heavin' that cable in, the wind howlin' like a bull. An' we had to come in wit' the flag at half-mast. On account of the two drowned men, you. That's always a sad sight, to see a vessel comin' in wit' the flag at half-mast. An' all the women on the shore just waitin', starin', not sayin' a word until the vessel's in and made fast and they know who it's for. But she was a good ship, you. She done good. She done famous."

But there was no escaping Auntie Pearl when she had her mind set on something.

"You've got it in that knapsack, haven't you now? Bring it out, girl."

April looked at Loren desperately, but he wasn't about to help her.

"Come on, now." Auntie Pearl was adamant. "Let's have a look."

April gave up. She pulled out her sketch pad and handed it to Auntie Pearl, who propped it up on the table in front of the boys.

Caleb stared. "That's some good!" he exclaimed.

Loren was surprised as well. This sketch was much more finished than the one of the cliffs. It showed the weather-beaten, grey frame house standing alone, with the old trees to one side of it, and the whole sweep of the island behind it. There was permanence and strength to the house, a feeling that it had stood in just this way for a hundred years, and would still be standing, just like this, a hundred years from now.

But it won't, Loren thought. Uncle Lem was so old now, he wouldn't be able to fish much longer. His son, Clarence, was so anxious to sell; all he needed was an excuse. The pie suddenly lay heavy in Loren's stomach.

"This dear girl says she'll give it to us when she's all finished with it," Auntie Pearl said. "Although I can't imagine what more it's needin'."

"Let me tell you," Uncle Lem continued, not really noticing the interruption, "by the time we made home I was right glad t'get back. Stuck with my father from then on, fishin' here from the island in our own boat. Although, you, whenever I saw them lovely white sails on the horizon...Well, I imagine I didn't just get t'yearnin' again. But I stayed. I stayed and never left for out wit' them again."

A far-away, almost wistful look had come over April's face. "They must have been beautiful, those old ships. I wish I could have seen them."

"Women goin' out in the boats all the time, now," Auntie Pearl bustled on, returning to her original subject. "You should go out with Caleb and Loren, here. I would've, when I was your age. Given the chance."

"I *would* like to go!" Then April hesitated and turned to Caleb. "But...I'd probably just be in the way...?"

Caleb shifted uneasily.

That's *all* we need, Loren thought bitterly. *April* out in the boat with us.

Suddenly, she grinned. "I know — maybe I could be *your* flunky/catchy. Like Uncle Lem. How about it?"

Caleb broke into an answering grin. "Why not? It might be fun."

"Hey! Just a second! Don't I get anything to say about this?" Loren glared at them. Uncle Lem and Auntie Pearl looked at him in surprise.

"Just what did you want to say, Loren?" There was a dangerous edge to April's voice.

"You've got a problem?" Caleb asked.

Loren flushed. Obviously neither of them cared a darn what he thought. "No," he answered shortly.

"Forget it. Why should *I* have a problem?" He said goodbye to Uncle Lem, thanked Auntie Pearl for the pie, and got up with Caleb and April as they made ready to go. He was outwardly calm, his face carefully blank, but inside he was seething.

Chapter 11

THE THREE OF them left together.

"No point taking the long way around," Loren said suddenly. "We might as well go the short way."

Caleb looked at him in surprise. "Over the Cannon Hole?"

"Why not?" Loren asked.

April looked at them curiously. "What's the Cannon Hole?"

"It's a cave. Under the cliffs. There's a path along the cliff edge above it, but it's not very safe…" Caleb said hesitantly.

"I've gone that way dozens of times," Loren retorted scornfully. "It's really a great place," he went on to April, ignoring Caleb. "We call it the Cannon Hole because when the tide is high the waves rush into it, pushing all the air in front of them. The air gets trapped in there, then sort of explodes and pushes the water back out. Sounds just like a cannon being fired."

"That's cool," April exclaimed. "Come on, Caleb, let's go."

Without waiting for Caleb's reply, Loren turned off the path and cut through the trees. April followed. Caleb seemed to hesitate, then finally came after them. When they came out of the trees on the cliff's edge, the path was barely a metre wide. Just as they emerged, a sharp boom split the air. April jumped.

"That's it," Loren said.

"Wow," April answered. "Impressive!"

"Look, the path narrows here," Loren said. "But all you have to do is hang on to the fence. Like this."

He went ahead, stepping carefully and hanging on with his left hand to a wire fence that ran along the forest side of the path, balancing his pail of fish in his right. Far below them the wild, spume-flecked waters raced into the cave and out again. Another boom shook the ground. Loren glanced back at April. She was following as closely as she could.

"Hang on!" he shouted.

"I am," she shouted back. "Believe me, I *am*!"

Loren paused for a minute, right in the middle, and looked deliberately down into the maelstrom. The sea seemed to ebb and flow beneath him, around him, right through him. His whole world, for that moment, was nothing but green, swirling water and noise. He felt a fierce surge of triumph and then an even greater sense of power.

They reached the other side. The path widened there, forming a broad shale shelf. April collapsed down on to it.

"That was awesome," she gasped. "Incredible!"

Loren looked back. Caleb still stood at the other side, his face white and pinched.

"Why is he waiting?" April asked.

Loren didn't answer.

Caleb took a step forward, slowly, onto the path, his gaze rivetted on the ground. Then, at the spot where Loren had paused, he stopped as well and, almost as if against his will, his eyes seemed to be drawn down to the water far below.

Loren made an involuntary movement towards him, his face suddenly twisted. "Caleb...No!"

As if pulled by a magnet, Caleb's body began to lean into the void. The fish bucket swung heavily outwards, and he with it. The only thing keeping him from toppling was his grasp on the fence. The bucket swung back and hit him on the legs. His knees buckled just as he lost his grip. The fish bucket bounced crazily from rock to rock into the insane fury of the waves. Fish scattered in a silver spray. Caleb recovered his balance but crouched, paralyzed.

Loren began to run.

"Loren!" April shouted. "What's the matter with Caleb?"

Just then Caleb's hand reached for the fence. Still staring down into the sea as if hypnotized, he pulled himself back up to his feet. Another boom rent the air. Caleb shuddered. Finally, he tore his eyes away and in one convulsive movement turned his back on the drop-off. With both hands hanging onto the fence, and small, sideways steps, he shuffled the rest of the way across.

"Caleb..." Loren began when he reached him.

Caleb silenced him with a look of pure hatred and strode past him down the path.

Loren was the only person on the island who knew Caleb's best-kept secret: he suffered from vertigo and was deathly afraid of heights. He could cope with the treehouse — just — but he had never before gone across the path over the Cannon Hole.

The next morning, when Loren went down to the wharf, there were two figures waiting for him. The boat was already off the slip and bobbing beside the wharf.

"You're not really going to take her, are you?" Loren burst out. Guilt made him even angrier than he had been the day before.

April, in jeans, a bulky sweater, and a lifejacket, stopped untying the painter and stared at him.

"She wants to go," Caleb answered shortly. "Why not?"

"But there's no place for her. She'll just be in the way."

"You're really nice, Loren," April shot back.

"Look," Caleb said. "She's going. If you've got a problem with that, why don't you just stay?"

"I'll do that!" Loren exploded. "You can't go out without me, and if she's going, I'm not." He whipped around and made for the path as fast as he could in all his awkward fishing gear.

See how he likes having to spend the day on shore when he could be out fishing, he fumed. But the engine of the Cape Islander coughed into life. The boat reversed, turned, and headed out to sea.

"Loren! What are you doing here? I thought you'd gone out with Caleb."

"I didn't go." Loren tried to move on past the study where his father was sitting.

"But I saw the boat go out. Who went with him?"

"April."

"April? She can't help with the boat. Why in the world didn't you go?"

"Ask Caleb. It was his idea, not mine." Loren turned to leave, but his father stopped him again.

"Now, Loren," he said, "I don't know what all's going on between you two, but Angus would have a fit if he knew."

"Not my fault," Loren answered sullenly. "I'm going upstairs."

"Wait a minute. There's something else I want to talk over with you."

"Not now, Dad. I..."

"I'm afraid it has to be now, Loren," his father replied. "I've received a letter from the Department of Transport."

Loren's heart sank.

"I'm being retired at the end of the summer, Loren. The lighthouse is going to be automated."

Loren whirled back around. "No!" he cried. "They can't!"

"They can. They have."

"Aren't you going to do anything about it?"

"There's nothing I can do." His father's voice was resigned. "The decision has been made."

"We can write! We can protest! I'll get all the men on the island to sign a petition saying they don't want the light automated. I'll get fishermen from the mainland to sign it, too." Loren towered over his father, furious. "There has to be *something* we can do!"

"Loren, things change. We have to accept that. We've both known this was coming." His father tried to put a hand on Loren's arm, but he shook it off.

"Well, I'*m* not going to accept it. *I'm* going to fight, even if you won't." Loren raced out of the room, took the stairs two at a time, and threw himself down at his desk. He'd write to the Department of Transport. He'd write to his member of Parliament. He'd write to anybody and everybody he could think of. He pulled out a pad of paper and began. When he finished that, he opened a drawer and pulled out the application forms for grade ten correspondence courses. Slashing at the pages, he filled them out, stuffed them in the envelope, and sealed it. His father could talk about accepting changes all he wanted, but this was Loren's home. This was where he had lived all his life, and this was where he was going to stay. If he had to fight for it, he would!

A sudden gust of wind slammed the window. As he got up to fasten the latch, Loren realized it was almost noon. The sun had gone behind some clouds and the wind was getting up from the east. They'll come in now, he thought. Caleb won't stay out with weather coming up like this.

The CB was buzzing in a corner of the kitchen when he came down for dinner, but there was no conversation. Then Uncle Forster's voice rang out.

"Seas are getting up, boys. I'll try one more shift and then I'll be headin' for in. You there, Caleb?"

"Yes, Uncle Forster. We're having pretty good luck

114

here — think I'll keep on for a while. It doesn't look too bad yet."

"Just you keep an eye out, you."

"I will."

"Good enough. Call you later."

Loren caught his father's eye, then looked quickly away as he slid into his place at the table.

His father had prepared a stew, thick with meat, potatoes and vegetables from the garden. Normally Loren would have wolfed down at least two full plates, but today he found he could hardly manage one. His father tried to make conversation, but Loren answered in monosyllables. He was concentrating on the CB, but aside from young Frank Parker coming on to announce disgustedly that there wasn't another fish left in the whole Atlantic so he was heading for in, the radio remained obstinately silent.

As soon as dinner was over Loren slipped out of the house. Young Frank had mentioned that he would be going over to West Harbour after he got back, and Loren wanted to give him his mail. By the time he reached the wharf, Uncle Frank's boat was just nosing into the harbour, with Uncle Lem and Clarence close behind. Loren looked out to sea, but there was no sign of Uncle Forster or Caleb. The wind was stronger now, and the ground seas were coming up, left over from a hurricane down around South Carolina earlier in the week. Ground seas and an easterly wind made for treacherous water. As he watched, another Cape Islander hove into view. Soon he could recognize the lines and bright red colour of Forster Landry's boat.

"Where's Caleb?" Loren asked as Uncle Forster

attached the haul-up hook to his boat.

"Oh, he should be headin' for in by now. Havin' too good a time out there to come in any sooner. When I passed I saw he's caught himself a boxful of fish — done better than the rest of us put together. And, would you believe it, that there girl is cuttin' and guttin' to beat the band. Who would've thought it?" He chortled as he threw the donkey engine into gear and his boat began to slide slowly up and out of the water. "I'm goin' over to the mainland with Frank and young Frank here — we'll send Caleb in right smart enough if he's still out there."

Loren gave them the letters, then watched as Uncle Frank's boat eased out of the harbour again. After helping Uncle Lem and Clarence unload their boat and secure it up on the slipway, he headed back towards his house. He walked into the kitchen just in time to hear Uncle Forster booming over the CB.

"Head for in, you foolish boy. Way the weather's comin' up, we may stay the night on the mainland, and you've no call to be out here alone. Angus wouldn't like it at all!"

"Good enough, Uncle Forster. Boat won't hold much more fish anyways." Caleb sounded confident and cheerful, perhaps just a trifle smug.

Probably hopes I'm listening, Loren thought bitterly. He turned and left the house again quickly. His feet led him towards the lighthouse and up the stairs. Automatically, his eyes swept the horizon, looking for boats. Uncle Forster and the others would have reached the mainland by now, but Caleb was not yet in sight. He must have been pretty far out, Loren thought. The sky was a dull grey, the sea a dark, greenish slate. Swells piled in, one after another.

Caleb should be in by now, Loren thought angrily. If he's going to take April out he should at least be a little careful. He strained to see the speck of a boat coming in until there were at least ten specks dancing in front of his eyes. And then it was there, riding the incoming seas and racing for the harbour. Loren could almost taste the sea water lashing his face, almost feel the exultation of the small speeding craft. He should have been out there. If it weren't for April...for Caleb's stubbornness...

All at once, amidst the froth of white water and spray enveloping the boat, a plume of black rose into the air. Thin and nebulous at first, it grew into a thick, wind-whipped column. Then a red lick of flame shot up from the wheelhouse.

Chapter 12

Loren tore down the narrow lighthouse stairs. Uncle Frank's boat was on the mainland. Uncle Lem Parker and Clarence were here, but their boat and Uncle Forster's were hauled up on the slipways. There was no time to launch either of them. No time even to go back to the house and alert his father. With any luck Caleb would have sent off a distress call on the CB, but he had to get out to them fast!

He dashed out onto the wharf, slipping on the damp planks. He untied the stern line and the painter, then leaped into the dory. He barely paused to make sure the fire extinguisher was in its usual place under the thwart, then yanked the starter cord frantically. He roared out of the harbour, bucking the swells. He was too low in the water to see Caleb's boat now, but that plume of smoke marked the spot. The fire extinguisher was poor comfort. Loren knew only too well how fast fire spreads on a boat — there wasn't any hope of getting there in time to fight it. If Caleb and April didn't get it out it would be all over by the time he got there. If the boat went down, at least he'd be there to pick them up.

The ground swells were enormous. Loren had to fight to keep the dory headed into them. In the troughs he couldn't even see the smoke from the burning boat, but each time he rose up to the top of a swell he could get his bearings. Finally, he saw the boat itself. He barely had time to see that there were no more flames and to catch sight of two figures in the stern; then he was down in another trough.

Just as he drew close enough to keep the boat in sight all the time, Caleb and April saw him. April waved frantically. Faintly, he could hear Caleb shouting. He hailed them back, then turned all his attention to pulling alongside.

"Caleb! Are you all right?"

"Loren!" Caleb called back. "I'm some glad to see you!"

Both their faces were smudged, and Caleb was holding one hand in front of him, cradling it on his other arm. The smoke, though, had disappeared. April was holding the boat's fire extinguisher.

"The fire's out," she shouted. "But Caleb's burned. We've got to get him back to shore."

"What about the boat?" Loren yelled.

"No good," Caleb answered. He seemed to be in considerable pain. "Nothing's working. There was a short in the bilge pump and by the time we got the fire out everything had gone. We can't start up the engine."

"The CB?"

"Gone, too. We never even had time to send a distress signal."

Loren maneuvred the dory so that he could keep alongside the Cape Islander, but not close enough to risk a collision. The wind was out of the east and they were considerably west of the island, but the dory was sturdy. With the five-horsepower outboard motor, he was pretty sure he could tow the Cape Islander home.

"I'll tow you," he called up. "April, catch the line!" Heading slightly away from the bigger boat, he picked up the coil of the stern line. With every ounce of strength he had, he threw it. The end fell into the stern of the Cape Islander. April grabbed for it. Caleb grabbed, too, but dropped it with a grimace of pain.

"Tie it to the ringbolt on the bow," Loren yelled.

April looked dubious. That meant sidling her way up past the wheelhouse on a narrow, slippery deck, while the boat wallowed and rolled in the swells. "I don't think I can...," she began.

"I'll do it," Caleb said.

"But your hand," she protested.

"Never mind. I can do it. Ever tied a decent knot in your life?" He made an effort to grin.

"Not one that stayed tied."

"Well, this one has to stay tied." Caleb took the line from her. His left hand was burned and useless to him, and he would need his right hand for hanging on, so he took the line and wrapped it several times around his left arm. He could just manage to hold the end of it gingerly between his thumb and forefinger.

Both Loren and April held their breath as the boat took a particularly violent roll, but Caleb grabbed for the window frame of the wheelhouse and hung on until the boat had again righted itself enough for him to continue. Finally, he made it to the bow and leaned over to tie the line onto the ringbolt that was used to haul the boat up. Loren tried to get the dory in close enough to help, but the seas made that impossible. He watched, almost in agony himself, as Caleb twisted the line and clumsily, painfully, tied a bowline. Then Caleb signalled to Loren to get under way.

The problem was going to be getting turned around. Loren steered carefully straight out and away from the Cape Islander until he felt the line come taut; then he began to come around into the wind. The dory bucked and rolled. He hardly dared take his eyes off the sea long enough to look back at the other boat. When he did, however, all seemed to be well. Caleb was in the bow, checking the line. Loren turned his attention back to the sea ahead. The dory ploughed on.

Suddenly there was a sharp bang. The motor quit. Instantly, the dory fell back. Frantically, Loren pulled the starter cord, praying that the engine would catch. But even when it did, the motor just raced uselessly — the propeller wasn't turning.

Loren tilted the motor, fighting against the tossing of the boat. The line was wrapped around the propeller. It had looped underwater while they were turning.

"Loren! What's the matter?" Caleb called.

Loren could barely hear him through the noise of the wind and the waves slapping against the dory. Feverishly, he began to untangle the line from the propeller.

"Sheared a pin!" he called back, not stopping to look up.

The line came free, but now what? The motor was useless. Loren unshipped a pair of oars and fitted them into the oarlocks, fighting to keep his balance in the crazily pitching dory, but there was no way he could tow the Cape Islander back to Windward Island by rowing. There was no way he could even make it back alone against the wind and in these seas. Desperately, he searched the bobbing horizon ahead. They should be close to Out Island. Yes — as he crested a swell he could see it dead ahead. With the wind behind them...

"The jigger-mast sail, Caleb! Put up the jigger-mast sail and make for Out Island!" His words were whipped away by the wind, but Caleb had obviously come to the same conclusion. He cast off the dory line. Loren could see him shouting to April. They rigged the small sail on the mast at the stern of the boat, and within seconds had it unfurled. Normally this sail was used to help the boat stand off from the net when they were at anchor, pursing the seine. It was not very big, but it would work.

Loren called over to the boat again. "April! Lean over here and grab an oar!" The dory was a double-hander and carried two sets. They could jury-rig a rudder from one of the extra oars.

Maneuvring as carefully as he could, Loren rowed alongside the Cape Islander. April reached down and grabbed the gunnel. It took all her strength just to hang on. Loren reached for one of the oars lying in the bottom of the boat and tipped it into the other boat.

"Good enough," Caleb called back. "I'll rig it up."

Loren let himself drift out of the way again and

watched anxiously as April and Caleb worked. Caleb's face was contorted with pain, but finally the sail was up and the oar lashed into place. April took over the makeshift rudder, and Caleb handled the sail. The boat tossed wildly. April looked terrified, but she hung onto the oar grimly. Then, before Loren could even call to them, Caleb got the boat under control, they came about, and were suddenly speeding away from him.

The wind coming from astern helped, but he still had to deal with the swells. Gradually, however, he made his peace with them, instead of fighting them. He rowed strongly up each towering hill, then eased up a little as he rowed down the other side, letting the wind and the force of the water help him as much as possible. Soon he had developed a rhythm. He lost track of how long he had been rowing, but when he finally looked back over his shoulder, Out Island was dead ahead. There was no sign of the Cape Islander, however, and he almost panicked. Then he realized that Caleb must have sailed around to the harbour on the lee side. The easterly wind was driving the waves onto the shore with tremendous force. They would never be able to anchor windward. It would be tricky, maneuvring into the western harbour, but Caleb could manage it, Loren was certain.

Sure enough, when he finally rounded the point, every muscle protesting, the Cape Islander was riding snugly at anchor out of the wind. Caleb and April were standing in the stern, scanning the harbour mouth anxiously. They waved when they saw him, but he was too exhausted to wave back.

Loren, Caleb and April stood in the Cape Islander; the dory, with its useless motor, rode peacefully alongside. Caleb had torn the tail off his shirt and wrapped it loosely around his burned hand. He was pale and his forehead was beaded with sweat in spite of the cool wind. Every freckle on his face stood out starkly.

April leaned, exhausted, against the wheelhouse. Behind her the cabin was a charred mess. The engine cover had nearly been burned through, and wires hung down from the radar and the CB. Dirty remnants of yellow foam covered just about everything. There was an acrid, electrical smell in the cabin. "What are we going to do?" Her voice wavered.

"Nothing tonight," Caleb answered. He slumped down onto the deck and leaned wearily against a lifejacket. "Wind's come up far too strong. Besides, it'll be dark soon. Don't want to be out rowing the dory in the ocean after dark, you."

"But we didn't get a message off on the CB and probably nobody but Loren saw the smoke. They won't know what's happened to us."

"They'll know something's wrong," Loren said. "Especially when Dad finds out I'm gone, too, with the dory. They'll come looking for us as soon as possible."

"Tide's low now, though," Caleb put in. "They won't be able to get the boats off the island, and Uncle Frank's is probably still on the mainland. They'll call the Coast Guard, I expect, but they're not likely to find us before nightfall."

Loren looked out towards the Brothers. He could just barely make out the islands through the heavy, looming clouds. The sun would be setting behind them now, he knew, but all they could tell of it was a gradual lessening of the light. The wind, however, had not lessened. Even in the harbour they could feel it. Out Island was little more than a big rock. The few trees on it were whipping back and forth. The only other things on the island were an automated lighthouse tower and the remains of the old fishermen's shacks.

"There's not much shelter on the island," Loren said. "I think we're better off on the boat for the night."

"On the boat? We're going to have to spend the night on the boat?" There was a note of hysteria in April's voice.

"Unless you can think of something better, we are," Loren answered shortly.

"We'll be perfectly safe," Caleb said more gently. "It's a good anchorage. In the morning, if need be, we'll go for help in the dory. They'll be out looking for us with the dawn, though — probably find us before we even wake up. We're better off to stay put here. We really are."

"But your hand, Caleb. It *can't* wait until tomorrow!"

"Guess it'll have to." Caleb closed his eyes and lay back with a sigh. Then his eyes flew open again. "Hey!" he said. "I know something we *can* do. We've still got lots of lunch left — let's eat!"

"Good idea," Loren answered. "Where is it?"

"In the wheel…Oh." Caleb looked chagrined. "It was sitting on the engine cover."

April walked in and pawed through the mess. She came out holding up a charred piece of bread.

"Toast?" she asked, her face dead serious. Then she burst out laughing, only it came out half laughter and half sobs.

Loren stared at the blackened scrap, dismayed. Then, in spite of himself, he began to laugh, too. It looked so ridiculous. Finally Caleb joined in. Helplessly, uncontrollably, with tears streaming down their faces, they laughed.

April tossed the bread over the side and sank down beside Caleb. She looked up at Loren, then started laughing again. "Oh, well. I was planning to go on a diet, anyway," she said.

"Speak for yourself," Loren answered. "I wasn't."

"At least we've got water," Caleb said. He reached down behind him and pulled out a thermos.

"Another thing we'd better do," Loren said finally, "is get rid of these." He gestured towards the fish boxes. "If we're going to have to stay here all night, I think I can do without their company."

"Get rid of them?" April asked.

"Yep. Over the side."

"Over the side? After all my hard work?"

"Afraid he's right." Caleb shrugged. "They won't be any good by the time we get them back to shore, anyway."

"Great. First time I do any *real* work and I've got to watch while it's all thrown out."

"Oh, no," Loren said mildly.

"What do you mean, 'Oh, no'? You're *not* going to throw them out?" April looked confused.

"No. I mean you don't have to watch. You have to help. I can't lift the boxes myself, and Caleb can't help with that bad hand. You're elected."

By the time they finished, the deck was covered with stray fish and guck. Caleb picked up as much as he could with his good hand and helped throw it all overboard. Finally, Loren grabbed a bucket and sluiced down the deck. April picked up a tin can and bailed the dirty water out. It was almost dark before they were through. They rewarded themselves with a sip each from the thermos. There wasn't much water left.

"Now for someplace comfortable to spend the night," Loren said. There were five lifejackets on board. He brought them into the wheelhouse. "We'll get a little shelter in here," he said. "We shouldn't be too cold." He didn't sound very certain. Caleb's face was white in the dusk. He was weaving as he tried to keep himself upright.

"Caleb, come on in here and sit down. You look awful." Loren led the way and settled Caleb on one lifejacket, with his back up against another. "You're in charge of the water," he said, handing Caleb the thermos. Then he made another nest out of two lifejackets for April.

With one last worried look at the night outside, she stumbled into the wheelhouse and burrowed into them.

"Loren?"

"Yes?"

"Are you sure we'll be all right here?"

"I'm sure. Try to go to sleep."

"Okay."

Loren settled himself beside Caleb, the remaining lifejacket cushioning his back. The cabin was pitch dark, and Loren was beginning to think the others had fallen asleep when Caleb's voice startled him.

"A lot of things have gone wrong, Loren, haven't they?"

"It wasn't your fault there was a short circuit," Loren answered quickly.

"I didn't mean that," Caleb answered. "Though I never should have taken the boat out without you. I was just so mad."

"You had every right to be." Loren stopped, searching painfully for the right words. "I should never have dared you to cross over the Cannon Hole like that. I knew...you could have been hurt...you could have been killed! But I was mad, too. I wanted to get back at you. I never thought you'd really try it, and then when you did..." He stopped again.

"What's happening, Loren?"

"I don't know." Loren stared into the black emptiness surrounding him. The words came with even more difficulty, slowly, one by one. "We've changed. We're growing different. I never thought that would happen."

"Me neither. I thought we'd always be the way we were."

Darkness settled between them again.

"I was sure glad to see you out there in that dory today, though," Caleb said. His voice was barely more than a whisper. As he spoke, he shifted his weight and let out an exclamation of pain.

Loren reached out instinctively. His hand closed on Caleb's arm. "I was sure glad to be there," he answered.

The boat rode easily at anchor, bobbing almost comfortably in the sheltered waters. Loren's grip tightened for a moment.

"Maybe we haven't done so badly after all," he said quietly.

"No," Caleb answered. "Maybe we haven't."

Chapter 13

LOREN WOKE UP feeling clammy and chilled right through to his bones. It took him a second to realize what it was that had awakened him; then he heard it again — the long, mournful note of the foghorn. At the same instant he realized he couldn't even see the stern. The boat, which had been riding peacefully in the lee of the harbour when he had gone to sleep, was now tugging at the anchor line. Although the wind had died down considerably, it must have shifted into the southwest. He felt a hand on his shoulder and heard Caleb's voice low in his ear.

"The wind's shifted. It's blowing onshore."

Out Island was rocky and treacherous here. If the anchor let go and they were blown onto the shore they would be dashed to pieces.

"Do you think we could move the boat around to the other harbour?" Loren knew the question was futile even as he asked it. They couldn't possibly sail directly into the wind with only their jigger sail. He thought about trying to tow them out with the dory, but he would never be able to do it. And in the fog the danger of the boat going aground or hitting a rock was just too great.

"No way," Caleb answered.

"What's...what's the matter?" April's voice was sleepy. Then she suddenly let out a cry. She clutched Loren's arm. "The fog! Oh, Loren, the fog! We're trapped!"

"April, it's okay. Really, it's okay." Loren reached out and grabbed her shoulders hard. He could just make out the pale oval of her face in the misty, not-quite-dawn light.

"But we're trapped! We can't see!"

Loren gave her a shake, then another as she started to sob.

"Stop it!"

She kept on sobbing, almost uncontrollably.

"Stop it!"

April slumped back against the lifejackets.

"We're okay, April," he repeated, trying to sound as normal as he could. "We're not trapped. We can get out."

"How?"

How indeed? Loren looked over to Caleb.

"They won't be able to find us in here with this fog," Caleb said slowly. "Not even with the radar."

"We've got the dory, though. We can't tow your boat, but we could row back to Windward Island. The wind'll be behind us once we get out of this harbour and around to the other side. Then we can come back with the others for your boat."

"I won't leave it."

"What?"

"I won't leave it. The anchor might let go, and if

131

there's no one on board she'll run onto the rocks and be lost."

"But you can't stay here. Your hand! You have to get back to shore as fast as possible."

"I've stood my hand this long, I guess I can stand it a little longer, you."

"But...can you manage the anchor line if you have to?"

"If I have to."

Loren moved to look at Caleb more closely. He was deathly pale. Black circles under his eyes seemed to be eating into his cheekbones. "You can't stay here, Caleb. Not alone. It's too dangerous."

"Well, I'm not going to lose my father's boat through my own foolishness."

"You did everything that could be done, Caleb. You can't blame yourself."

"Whatever. I'm not going to leave this boat."

April had her arms wrapped around her body as if she were holding herself together. "Loren, you're not going to row out into that fog!"

"I can't just sit here. They won't find us until the fog lifts, and that could take hours. Caleb needs help as soon as possible." He knew Caleb's mind was made up and there would be no budging him. Caleb was right, too. With no one on board, the chances of losing the boat were high. But even with Caleb on board...weak and in pain, one hand almost useless...

"Go, Loren. You've got to go. It's the only way."

"What about me?" April sounded desperate.

"The dory's a double-hander," Loren answered. "If you row with me we can make it back to the island twice as fast."

"But if I stay here I can help Caleb if he needs it."

"You couldn't help much." Caleb's voice was rough.

Loren knew Caleb was thinking about what might happen if the anchor didn't hold. It was too dangerous for her to stay, and they could get to help much more quickly if she came with him.

"Come with me, April," he said. "Really, that would be best."

"Loren — I can't! I can't row out into that fog! I can't, Loren."

"You have to. I need you to row, and Caleb needs us to get help for him as soon as possible. You've got to."

For a long moment April just stared. Then, tentatively, she reached up a hand. Loren helped her to her feet. She was shaking so hard that she stumbled twice getting to the stern of the boat.

Loren got into the dory first, then held it close to the Cape Islander as steadily as he could while April clambered in. She took her place in the bow, clutching the thwart while Loren fixed the long wooden oars into the oarlocks. A sudden thought struck him.

"Have you ever rowed before?"

"*Now* you ask me. Yes. I hated it."

"Well, hate it or no, it's going to come in handy. Let's see how strong you are. You thought you did so well with those fish yesterday; let's see how well you can do with this."

He let go of the side of the Cape Islander, and by the time he had fixed his own oars in place they had drifted almost out of sight of it.

"Are you all right, then?" Caleb called anxiously.

His voice was already muffled by the fog.

"Fine," Loren called back. "We're on our way."

"Good enough!"

One last glimpse of Caleb's face, staring after them as they rowed past the boat, then they were alone in the fog.

"Loren!" April sounded frantic. "We can't see *anything* out here!" She was huddled on the thwart behind him, hanging on to the oars desperately, but making no attempt to row.

"Listen for the foghorn," he said. "That's what it's there for. We'll just keep heading for it and we'll be fine. Row with me, April. Row!"

The most dangerous part was right now — getting out of the harbour. It was easy to get mixed up in fog. Loren kept the wind at his back and rowed with long, easy strokes, keeping his eyes fixed on the spot where he had last seen Caleb. Five minutes should put them well outside the harbour. Already, he could hear the sound of the buoy that marked the entrance. He made straight for it and almost ran it down. He rounded it and headed east. Just faintly, reflected through the fog, he could make out the light at the eastern tip of Out Island. Once past that he could head directly towards the foghorn. They should be able to make it. Should be...

The Out Island light disappeared into the fog. With the wind helping now, Loren settled into a rhythm. His arm muscles had protested painfully at first, but by now they had loosened up. To Loren's immense surprise and relief, after a jerky, confused start, April fell into his pattern and began to row with him steadily and strongly.

"You're doing great!" he shouted over his shoulder, but there was no answer and he didn't want to break his rhythm by turning around again.

The waves gradually smoothed out and the choppiness diminished. The fog seemed to be dissipating, too. The foghorn moaned regularly, faithfully. Loren had no way of estimating how far they had come, but it sounded closer and closer.

April's oars faltered. Loren stopped rowing and glanced back over his shoulder. She still looked scared, but her mouth was clamped into a thin, determined line.

"Are you all right?" he called.

She closed her eyes and leaned over the oars. "My hands are sore. How much longer, Loren?"

"Not too long. Hear how close the foghorn is now? We're getting there, April. We're getting there. Okay?"

She shook her head — it could have meant yes or no. Then she started rowing again.

After what seemed like an interminable length of time, however, they were still rowing, still alone in the fog. Loren looked back over his shoulder again and again, staring into the grey curtain, willing the shape of Windward Island to emerge. April's oars were skipping more often than not, and she wasn't keeping up. Surely he should be picking up the light by now, even through the fog. Then, off to port, he heard a sound. A moan — then another. It was the Groaner. Well to port. Old Grampus reef was over there and they were dead on course. With renewed energy he tackled the oars again. April seemed to sense his eagerness and she began keeping up with him again.

With the reef safely behind him, Loren angled directly towards the island. He willed himself not to look around again until he was sure he must be close to the shore. He could almost imagine he heard the waves breaking on the cliffs. Finally, he allowed himself to turn around. Nothing. He strained his eyes and then, almost as if by his own sheer relentlessness, the fog wavered and began to lift. Suddenly, in the last faintly dark hour of the dawn, a beam of light broke through. Three flashes and a pause. Three flashes and a pause.

"April!" Loren cried. "Look! The light — "

April whipped around, then turned quickly back to Loren. Her face was soaking wet — whether with tears or spray or both, he couldn't tell — but she was smiling radiantly. "I see it, Loren! I *see* it!"

They bent to the oars and the fog continued to lift. The next time Loren looked over his shoulder the blinking light of the harbour buoy was in sight. He rounded it, and felt the full surge of the incoming tide helping them race into the harbour mouth.

As soon as they were alongside the wharf April leaped out to tie the painter to the ringbolt.

"Loren, we made it!" She was definitely crying now, tears pouring down her face, but laughing, too. "In the fog! We made it!" As Loren stepped up onto the wharf she threw her arms around him in an enormous bear hug. "Oh, that light! I've never seen anything so wonderful in my life!"

Loren hugged her back as two figures loomed up

out of the remnants of the fog. Uncle Lem Parker and Clarence were coming down the path.

"Loren!" Uncle Lem exclaimed. "What are you doin' here, boy? Where's Caleb, then?"

"What happened?" Clarence asked. "We've been some worried about you all. Where's the boat?"

The questions tumbled over Loren. "Caleb's with the boat," he answered, "but there was a fire. It's disabled. Caleb managed to get it into the western harbour of Out Island, but he wouldn't leave it because the wind's onshore and he was afraid the anchor wouldn't hold. We've got to get back to him."

"Well, the wind's died down enough now," Uncle Lem said. "He should be all right, but we'll get out t'him as fast as possible, you. We was just waitin' for the fog t'lift to get the boat goin'."

"The others have already set out from the mainland," Clarence put in. "I'll get on the CB and tell them where to go and we'll meet them there."

Uncle Lem was shaking his head as if he still couldn't believe that they were actually standing there. He broke into a huge smile. "It's *some* good t'see you!"

"Annie — just sick she was," Clarence said. "But she wouldn't call Angus. 'Not 'till morning,' she said. 'I won't have him lying awake all night worrying.' Course that's just what she's been doing herself, mind, although I'd wager she didn't do much lying down!" He headed for the boat, calling over his shoulder as he went. "Your father's been monitoring the CB steady since yesterday, Loren. Is it gone, too, then?"

"Yes," Loren answered. "Everything."

"*Your* father's had half the Coast Guard out all

137

night lookin' for you, April," Uncle Lem said. "Never saw a man so distracted in all m'life. Insisted on coming out with us this mornin', too, although I told him there was no need. He'd be just as well off here. Wouldn't take no for an answer, though. He'll be along any minute."

"*My* father? *That* worried?"

"Sure was."

Dan Lohnes rounded the bend in the path. "Clarence…," he began, then he saw April and Loren.

"April!" He broke into a run but stopped, awkwardly. "April!" he repeated. He held out his hands, almost in a pleading gesture.

April's face closed and hardened the moment she saw him. She stood, immobile. Then, slowly, almost fearfully, she reached out her hands towards him.

He grasped them. His fingers tightened around hers and he beamed down at her. He suddenly looked years younger. "Thank God you're safe, April," he breathed. "I couldn't have borne it if I had lost you, too."

As if a light had been turned on, April's face lit up. "I'm okay, Dad," she answered. "We all are."

"Loren, help me with the lines here," Clarence called.

"We've got to get back to Caleb," April said, but she was still staring into her father's eyes as if she couldn't believe what she saw there.

He released her and gave her a rough, embarrassed hug. "You go on. I'll tell your father the good news, Loren. And Annie. They'll sure be glad to hear it."

"You'd better get on to the Coast Guard, too," Uncle Lem said. " 'Case I can't raise 'em on the CB."

"You're coming with us?" Loren asked.

"I sure am," April answered.

"In Uncle Lem's boat?"

"Well, I wasn't planning on swimming, and I've had enough rowing for a lifetime."

"But it's still foggy — you don't mind?"

"Fog? Pooh. What's a little fog?" April grinned. "Take more than that to scare *me*."

Loren grinned as well. "Come on, then. Let's go!"

Chapter 14

"THAT WAS *SOME* good sight, seeing you all rounding the point into that harbour," Caleb said.

Caleb, April and Loren were stretched out in the treehouse living room, comfortably munching on steamed mussels. Caleb held his neatly bandaged hand carefully in his lap.

"That was *some* good sight, seeing you still there safe and sound," Loren answered.

"That's for sure," April agreed. She had been formally invited this time by Caleb *and* Loren. "How's Uncle Angus? Did you see him this morning?"

"Yes. He's doing fine. Be out in another week, I think." Caleb looked at her intently. "How's your dad? He seemed a lot happier when he was over for dinner last night."

The light went on in April's face again. "Isn't it fantastic? He's like a different person! That night — after we all got back, you know? We sat up and talked for hours. It was so great! I told him about my drawing — showed him some stuff — and *he* said I should take lessons. We even talked about Mom..." She paused, then went on. "He told me things about her I'd never known. About when she was young and they first met. About when they decided to leave the island and live on the mainland. About when she was first starting to paint. He said I was good — just as good as she was then." April's eyes were shining with pride.

"Is it true you're leaving this week?" Loren's words sounded gruff.

"Dad is. He wants to get back to work. Says he's glad he came here — so am I! — but it's time to 'get on with things.' I think he's really, finally going to be able to cope. Aunt Annie asked me if I'd like to stay until school starts, though, and I said I would. So I guess you'll have to put up with me for a little longer," she added with a sideways glance at Loren.

Loren was surprised at the jolt of happiness that ran through him. "Oh, I guess I can bear it," he said lightly.

April suddenly turned shy. She looked down at her hands in her lap and twisted a ring on one of her fingers, then took a deep breath. "I, uh...I brought something with me for you two." She fumbled in the knapsack at her feet and brought out two carefully rolled sheets of drawing paper. She handed one each to Caleb and Loren. "They're not so great, you know, but I thought...well...I thought you might like them."

Caleb unrolled his first. It was a charcoal sketch of him in profile — just his head and shoulders — at the wheel of the Cape Islander. His eyes were looking far ahead and his short, red hair was slicked back and wet with spray. Caleb stared at it, speechless. It was an incredibly good likeness, but there was also a hint of something — just a suggestion of an older, more mature Caleb.

"That's great!" Loren exclaimed. Then he and April both burst into laughter as they watched Caleb turn a dark, painful beet red.

"I don't know what…" Caleb stuttered. "What can I say? Thank you!" he finally managed to get out.

"I bought some charcoals when we went into town that day, and then just watched you on the way back. When I wasn't busy being scared to death, I mean," April said, still laughing. "Now you, Loren," she went on. "Look at yours."

Slowly, Loren unrolled his sheet. There was the sketch of the easternmost point – his favourite place – but now it was a polished and powerful drawing.

"That's what I was doing when I got lost in the fog. I'd gone back to finish, and then fell asleep like the turkey I am," April said. "Do you like it?"

Loren looked at it. The drawing spoke to him of everything he felt and loved about the island. Of everything he feared losing. There were no words to describe how much it moved him. Finally, he just looked back at April. "Oh, yes," he said. "I like it." She smiled, and he smiled back.

"Look, you guys." April turned to include Caleb. "When you go to school on the mainland – Halifax isn't all that far away, you know. Will you come and visit me? Aunt Annie's already said I can come back here any time I want."

"We sure will," Caleb answered. "Think your Dad's friend would take us out on his boat?"

April laughed. "He'll have you out in it the whole

time you're there, if you want. It's his pride and joy."

Loren looked at them. The happiness he had been feeling suddenly drained away and was replaced by a leaden coldness. Just like that, they were both assuming that he would be going to the mainland to go to school. That he would leave the island. But up in his room, on his desk, sat the first installment of his correspondence course lessons.

When he got home his father was sitting up in the kitchen, waiting for him. "We need to make a decision, Loren." he said. "We can't put it off any longer."

Loren put out a hand and braced himself against the door frame.

"My retirement date has come through. August." His father waited a moment, but Loren couldn't answer. "Mr. McIvor was around this afternoon. He wants the house."

Too much. Too sudden. I can't take this, Loren thought, and exploded into words. "No! You can't sell! You didn't…!"

"I haven't given him any answer yet. I wanted to talk it over with you first. But we have to, Loren. Once I'm retired we'll have to live on the mainland, and I'll need the money from this house to buy us something over there."

His father looked at Loren steadily. Loren couldn't meet his eyes. With all his heart he wanted to shout the loudest refusal he could and slam out of the kitchen. Take refuge in his own room and shut the door against everything. But this time he couldn't. This time that wouldn't solve anything.

"We'll still come back to visit, Loren. Angus will still be here — and Dan Lohnes says that now they've got the house fixed up he and April will come back from time to time."

"Visit?" The word was bitter. "You don't *visit* your home — you *live* there."

Suddenly his father seemed to sag in his chair. "It's been my home, too, Loren. For over sixty years. When I leave here I'll be leaving my whole lifetime of memories...I can't bear it any more than you can, son. And I can't bear it alone."

Loren was kneeling at his side in an instant. To his horror he found his eyes filling with tears. He laid his head on his father's lap, as he had done when he was very little and had been hurt — and he cried. His father's hands soothed him and stroked his hair, just as they had all those years ago. Like the small boy he had been in those bygone days, Loren put his arms around his father's knees and held on tight.

It was one of those typical late August days when the skies are a clear blue with cumulus clouds piled high. The setting sun reflected off the water in splinters that made Loren squint. He was standing in the stern of Uncle Angus's boat, bracing his feet against the roll and pitch of the waves.

Ahead of him lay the mainland, the neat shingled cottage he and his father had bought, and high school. A new life. Not for him, now, the job of lightkeeper. Not for anyone on Windward Island ever again. He had fought, but he had lost. The light was automated; the island was going to change. But the island would still be there. And the sea. And the birds. And he would be back.

The sun was sinking quickly, racing down over the horizon behind the Brothers as the Cape Islander ploughed on. Loren turned for one last look. As he watched, the houses dwindled out of sight, the outline of the island became hazy in the gathering dusk. Finally, all he could see was the light. Three flashes and a pause. Three flashes and a pause. And then even that became only a memory.